W9-BPL-076

Bedford High School
Library

Escape the Mask

ESCAPE

THE GRASSLAND TRILOGY

THE MASK

DAVID WARD

AMULET BOOKS
NEW YORK

PUBLISHER'S NOTE: This is a work of fiction. Names, characters, places, and incidents are either the product of the author's imagination or are used fictitiously, and any resemblance to actual persons, living or dead, business establishments, events, or locales is entirely coincidental.

Library of Congress Cataloging-in-Publication Data:

Ward, David, 1961–
Escape the mask / David Ward.
p. cm. — (The grassland trilogy; bk. one)
Summary: Six young friends, tortured by the Spears and forced to work as slaves in the harsh fields of Grassland, vow to escape to find the freedom that was stolen from them long ago, and their opportunity arises when Outsiders come and wage war against the Spears.
Hardcover ISBN: 978-0-8109-9477-5
[1. Slavery—Fiction. 2. Torture—Fiction. 3. Science fiction.] I. Title.

PZ7.W1873Esc 2008
[Fic]—dc22
2007028212
Paperback ISBN: 978-0-8109-7990-1

Text copyright © 2001, 2009 David Ward
First published by Scholastic Canada Ltd.
Published in hardcover by Amulet Books in 2008.
Map by Paul Heersink/Paperglyphs

Book design by Chad W. Beckerman

Published in 2009 by Amulet Books, an imprint of Harry N. Abrams, Inc. All rights reserved. No portion of this book may be reproduced, stored in a retrieval system, or transmitted in any form or by any means, mechanical, electronic, photocopying, recording, or otherwise, without written permission from the publisher. Amulet Books and Amulet Paperbacks are registered trademarks of Harry N. Abrams, Inc.

Printed and bound in U.S.A.
10 9 8 7 6 5 4 3 2 1

Amulet Books are available at special discounts when purchased in quantity for premiums and promotions as well as fundraising or educational use. Special editions can also be created to specification. For details, contact specialmarkets@hnabooks.com or the address below.

harry n. abrams, inc.
a subsidiary of La Martinière Groupe
115 West 18th Street
New York, NY 10011
www.hnabooks.com

For Holly

Thanks to Dr. Gunderson
and Dr. Leggo; Jackie Siedel;
Mike Barker; Tracy Zuber;
my agent, Scott Treimel;
Sandra Bogart Johnston; and
the team at Amulet Books
for being captured by Grassland.

Desert
To the Grove
Spear Village
Graveyard
Main road to caves
Stream Trees

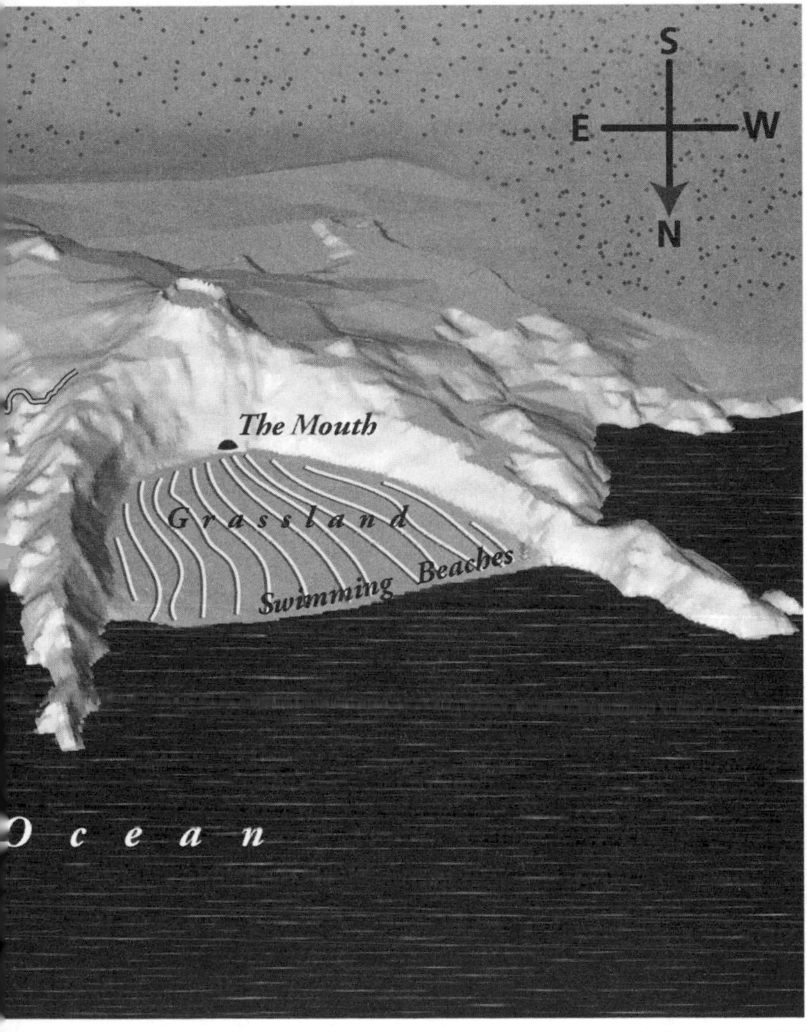

S
E
W
N
The Mouth
Grassland
Swimming Beaches
Ocean

I

THERE WAS FEAR COMING FROM the Onesies' cages. With each new outbreak of moaning it blew across my bare skin like a chill wind from the lower caves. I could smell their dust and the waft of drying sweat from such a long journey across the sands. Thirst and desert is all they would have known for many days, since it is impossible to see the ocean until you have passed through the caves and come to the other side. But that all changes with the First Cleansing.

I was lucky not to be locked up with them. One night in the cages beside the Onesies is what I got for bringing a work-cloth into the cell. I shook my head in admiration that Pippa had been right again. She was angry with me in the beginning, but more because I had been caught than because I had tried.

"Stupid, Corki. Stupid," she had scolded the moment the Spears left our cell. "Now you have a night of fear to look forward to." She folded her arms. "And me . . . a night of loneliness." The cut on her leg was deep and the extra cloth was needed to staunch the bleeding. We both knew it was worth the risk. Blood brought the Spears into the cells faster than an early morning run toward the beach. She had braided my hair until they came to take me to the cages.

I touched the plaits sliding across my back and fingered the tight knots her nimble hands had made. Pippa's plaits were famous in Grassland and had saved me many beatings from stronger boys. I smiled as I thought of her flashing eyes and wished again for the hundredth time that she was lying next to me.

A hissing sound from somewhere above stirred my thinking. With no further warning the torchlight of the cave flickered out, leaving us in total darkness.

The Onesies all screeched at once. I threw my hands over my ears, partly to stop the roaring echoes that vibrated throughout the caves, but more importantly, to hide from their terror. Shuddering, I pulled one of my braids around to my mouth and sucked on it. When the sobbing finally settled I shut my eyes as well and imagined the sunlight, the high grasses, the ceaseless ocean, and Pippa's warm breath on the back of my neck. It would be cold tonight, especially after the First Cleansing.

The Spears always waited until the new captives were asleep, exhausted from the long march and from the constant fear. Then the water would come, slowly at first, enough to startle the youngest awake. Dribbles across the floor would turn to streams, and streams to torrents, until every cage in the lower caves was flooded, exposed fully to the ocean tunnels. The weak would drown. The strong would be broken completely, ready to do whatever they were told after a cold night of shivering beside dead companions.

"Help, oh Mommy, Mommy," someone was crying in the cage nearest me. Voices from the North were rare, and I couldn't stop myself from taking my hands away from my ears to listen. "What are we going to do?" It was a boy, probably close to my age, although terror always made it hard to tell.

"Shhh. Let me listen." A girl this time, and definitely

older. "Sit up against the back wall and lean against me." There was a shuffling and I heard the boy groan.

"No," I whispered. "Sit up close to the bars and hold on tight."

"Who are you?" the girl called back, more loudly than I liked.

I ignored her. "Sit up against the bars, the ones closest to me, and wrap your legs around them. That way you can face what is coming. When the water comes, turn sideways and keep your head up as high as you can. Hold your breath when you need to. The ocean comes in surges."

"What ocean?" the boy asked.

"You'll see."

"What's going to happen?" The boy's voice was shaking and, for once, that was a good thing. Fear might save them if they did what I told them.

"Don't talk anymore," I hissed. "You'll bring the Spears." They fell silent and I heard them both moving their positions across the stone floor. I wrapped one arm around my chest, the other around the center bar of my cage, and rested fitfully, waiting.

• • •

The First Cleansing came as it always did. When the first cold trickles splashed against my legs, I sat up as high as the top bars would allow and tilted my head toward the ceiling. I could hear the boy and girl stirring now.

"What is happening?"

"Do as I told you!" I yelled. There was no risk talking now. The Spears had to leave the caves before the water was let in. "Wrap your legs around the bars and turn sideways. Sit up, high!"

"Please tell us what is going on!" the girl cried out.

I gripped the bars a little tighter. "This is the First Cleansing. It is always the worst. They let the ocean pour into the cages."

"Are we going to *drown*?" The boy's voice was winding into a frenzy. Around us the rush of the water was getting louder.

"Not if you keep sideways. Don't face the water, or it will knock you to the back of the cage. That is how most die. If you lose your grip and fall away, hold your breath and wait for the ebb flow to suck you back against the front bars, then grab on again. Don't miss."

They were both weeping now, their voices joined by

dozens of others, calling out in their various languages, trying to stay above the rising streams. My own blood began pumping faster, despite the fact that I'd lived through four First Cleansings already.

"Don't forget what I said," I yelled again. Although I had no loyalty to anyone other than Pippa, I felt sorry for these two. They spoke my language and they were afraid. Pippa would have helped them. "Pretend you are swimming. It is a game. All is well?"

"All is well," the girl shouted back hoarsely.

There was a slight change in the echoes around us, and for a brief moment the rush of the water slackened. I immediately wrapped my leg around the bar.

"Here it comes."

A blast of warm air blew my hair straight back as a solid wave of ocean pushed a rushing wind ahead of it. The water hit me hard, like a punch from a Spear, and filled the entire cage faster than I had remembered. I was in pitch darkness and under cold ocean that grabbed like claws to lift my fingers away from the bars and pummel me against the wall of the cage. I held my breath and forced myself to think of Pippa and not give in to fear. I could feel the slimy bodies of small fish smash against my sides, and I cringed in pain as some sharp object struck my shoulder. Then the surge suddenly burst, rebounding against the far wall, and I was sucked back against the bars as the water receded. After that first swell it seemed like forever before my head came above the surface again.

I sucked in deep, delicious breaths of air and waited, happily leaning against the cold metal bars until the waves receded as quickly as they had come. Only one more to go. Choking and screaming were coming from all over. I hoped that the boy and girl were still alive.

"Are you all right?" I shouted in the lull.

"Still here," the girl called back. Although she was breathless and afraid, there was a note of determination that had not been there before.

"You're going to make it. There is only one more."

"I don't know if my brother can do it."

"Put him in front of you and wrap your arms around his chest. Make sure he is holding on to the bars as well." Pippa and I had survived several First Cleansings this way. She was not as strong as I was, so we had to find a method of helping her last through the two surges. As always, she had come up with the idea. "Do it quickly. The water won't wait for you."

I never found the second wave as bad. Even when I had to hold Pippa in front of me, I always felt as if we had beaten the Spears by being alive after the initial surge. But this wasn't my first time, either.

When the air rushed toward us once again, I called out one more time, "Hold on tight. You will make it!" My shoulder was aching from whatever it was that had hit it. As the water rushed over my head I found myself wondering if there was blood.

I held my breath for a long time, counting, waiting for the swell to recede. *Pippa's hands counting down, ten . . . nine . . . eight . . .* And then it was over.

I shook my braids and immediately knelt on the floor to feel for anything tasty that the sea might have left behind. Other than a slimy piece of weed there was nothing, and I cursed my luck. Torchlight suddenly appeared and I glanced up at the cage of the boy and girl. They were still clinging to the cage bars, with the girl behind, supporting her brother.

Her head turned toward me. When our eyes met,

she suddenly released herself, allowing both of them to fall backward onto the floor. The boy went into a fit of coughing, but the girl continued to stare up at me. I stood as tall as I could and shuffled to the end of the cage so I could see them better.

The first shock I had was that they both had dark hair, though their accents were the same as mine. Pippa and I were as blond as the tops of the sweet grasses in the noon sun. White Eye, the only other who had spoken our language, had been fair-haired like us, not dark like these newcomers.

She poked at the boy. He sat up, pulled away from her, and turned to me.

"Is the water going to come again?" he asked between spasms of coughing.

"No. Not tonight. In fact, never again unless you break the rules. All the other Cleansings are easy and feel good when they come."

"Why were *you* here?" the girl asked.

"I brought a work-cloth into our cell."

"And that's wrong?"

"Only if you get caught."

The girl continued to stare, then dropped her eyes to the floor. Her face turned slightly red. "Are they going to take our clothes and make us wear what you have?"

"Yes."

She nodded. "Thank you for telling us what to do."

I liked these two. The boy was trying hard to live, and other than his hair he made me think of me. The girl was mysterious. She was probably the oldest female I had ever seen, and I was surprised they had let her into the caves. She reminded me of someone from long ago, someone who used to sing . . .

"What is your name?" she asked.

"I am Coriko. My mate is Pippa."

The girl raised her eyebrows and a smile curved on her lips. "Your *mate*? How old are you?"

"I don't know how old I am. Pippa thinks we are twelve or thirteen summers."

"And she is your mate?"

I nodded. "My cell mate."

Her smile widened. "Ohhh. I think I understand now."

There were heavy footsteps behind us. I instinctively

held up two fingers, forgetting that Onesies wouldn't know our hand signals. "Be quiet now," I said. Just before the shadows of the Spears flickered on the walls of the tunnel, I whispered, "What are you called?"

"I am Tia," the girl said.

"I am Bran," the boy called too loudly. The sound echoed past me. We fell silent.

The Spears stepped quickly, in twos as always. As they approached our cages I noticed a red mark, in the shape of a closed fist, on some of their chests. These were different from the Spears who watched us in the fields. I had seen the red fist only on Spears who brought Cleansings and punishments. But like any other Spears, their black helmets glinted dully and their frowning masks showed no emotion for what they were about to do.

I stepped back from the bars and put my hands out wide from my sides while the Spears unlocked the latches. The Onesies didn't know the custom. Out of the corner of my eye I watched a Spear thrust the butt end of his prod through the bars and into Tia's stomach as she tried to protect Bran. She doubled over and the door was unlocked. They left only one Spear to watch me. They had no intention of opening my cage until it was time for me to leave in the morning.

I looked on as they entered my new friends' cage. The first Spear grabbed Tia by her long dark hair and pulled her up from her retching position. She began to struggle, and Bran brought his leg back to kick.

"Don't fight!" I hissed. "Just stand still. They won't hurt you if you don't move."

Tia stopped immediately and Bran held his kick in check, never taking his eyes off his attackers. The Spear holding Tia's hair raised a knife and Bran shot a fast glance back in my direction.

"Peace, be still," I shouted as calmly as I could above the screams of others. Tia stood facing me, her eyes fixed on mine, wide but trusting. There was a shredding sound and the top of her garment fell to her waist. With another rough tear the Spear pulled the remaining clothes from her body. She stood shaking as if the floor were moving.

Then the Spear moved on to Bran, gripping his hair the same way he had Tia's, and removed his garments in a single swipe. The clothes were picked up by the second Spear, who gave Tia and Bran a quick shove into the back of the cage before slamming the bars into place. Two cell wraps, hoodless and gray like my own, were tossed in. Then the Spears moved on.

Tia was weeping softly. Bran gripped the bars and yelled after the retreating Spears.

"Say nothing more!" I whispered. "They have come back before, and they don't forgive."

His eyes suddenly watered and he stared at me hopelessly.

"Go to sleep, Bran," I whispered one more time. "And put on your cell wraps."

He allowed his sister to pull him down beside her. They put on their new clothes and the difference was startling. Other than Tia's height they looked like the rest of us.

In the torchlight I could see at least three cages down from mine. I shook my head in disbelief. What was going on? There were older boys in the group as well. One of them even had a little hair on his face. Why bring captives this old?

I shrugged and lay down in the center of the floor, careful to avoid my shoulder. Tia and Bran would be well for the rest of the night—if they managed to get any sleep with all the moaning and bone-chilling cold. I closed my eyes, drowning out the grief, the pain, the death, in the cages so near.

"Good night, Pippa," I whispered to the stony ceiling above me.

All night long a Spear ran the butt of his prod across the bars as he passed, a constant reminder that we were not alone.

2

MORNING CAME WITH THE low drone of a conch shell blowing down the length of the tunnel. I stood slowly and stepped back to the wall, my arms moving out to my sides to show that I was ready to leave. I glanced at Tia and Bran and watched them move to the back of their own cage. They were learning fast. Tia smiled at me awkwardly and nodded a greeting.

Bran wanted to say something. He made eye contact with me, but I shook my head, no. My cage would be the first to open, since I was a Twosie and would be sent to the far fields, away from the Onesies. The Spear unlocked my bars and I stepped out. I bowed briefly, then moved toward the Mouth Tunnel with his heavy footsteps right behind me. I wondered if I would see my new friends again.

The light grew brighter toward the opening of the Mouth and I squinted at its intensity. Another Spear handed me a work-cloth, which I had to put on slowly, because of my aching shoulder. As I pushed my head through the neck and my shoulders through the arm holes, I tried to make my movements look natural, as if I was tired, nothing more. But I needn't have worried. The frowning mask was turned away from me, concerned with something going on farther down the tunnel. The Twosies had been in the fields for a while already, and I could feel my anticipation rise at the thought of seeing Pippa.

The Spear led me from the Mouth along the narrow, well-trodden path I had walked for years. I knew every dip, every outcrop, in the steep slopes that ran along either side. I smelled the dewy grasslands in a single breath and stared out across the fiery yellow stalks to the sea. Behind me the towering mountains surrounded a perfect half circle of grasslands and beach. Beyond them the ocean gleamed. In the late afternoon it would creep forward to cover the grass and sand. The shadow of the mountains stretched far out over the grasses, reaching halfway to the water, and I pulled my work-cloth around me tighter until we broke out into the sun. It was cool now, but by noon I would need the hood to protect me from its rays.

At the first mark, the Spear stepped into the shade of a high shelter. It was made by tall poles driven into the sand, with a patchwork of cloths stretched into a rough square above. I walked to the diggings by myself. Everyone stared as I passed, some pausing long enough to sneer, while others gave encouraging smiles. One boy signed Friendship with an open palm.

I sighted Pippa's blond hair from many paces away, but her wild wave told me she had already seen me. I tried not to run the last hundred strides of our furrow, but if I was worried about making a scene, Pippa certainly wasn't. She jumped the last few steps, wrapping her legs around my waist and knocking me down onto the soft sand. When the wind came back into my lungs I opened my eyes and stared up into her laughing face.

She kissed my nose. "I missed you," she whispered.

"I missed you, too." Her cheek had a smudge of dirt from where she had wiped at a fly or a drop of sweat, and I brushed at it with my clean hand. "I have so many things to tell you."

Her laughter was gone. "Do not go away from me again."

"I won't."

"Not ever, Corki."

"Not ever," I repeated. My eyes traveled over her sun-browned face and I tried to hide a smile. I had said the same thing a little while ago and I was hoping she hadn't remembered. She rolled off of me and I groaned at the pressure on my shoulder.

"What happened?"

"I got hurt during the Cleansing."

She sat up and scanned above the knee-high stalks before turning back to my arm. As long as we reached our quota of shards, it didn't matter what we did in the fields because the Spears rarely moved out into the sunlight except to break up a fight or wake a careless sleeper. They never came out at midday. But it wasn't wise to let the other Diggers see weakness of any kind.

She felt the back of my shoulder. "There is nothing, just bruising, I think." I could feel her small hands searching, probing for blood or an open sore of any kind.

"You should have told me. I would not have jumped."

"You would have jumped anyway."

Her green eyes flashed and she kissed my nose again. "Was it bad this time?"

I shrugged. "Same, except for my shoulder."

"I prayed for you."

"I know. How is your leg?"

She held her leg up for my inspection. "It stopped bleeding last night. I put a lot of spit on it and that seemed to help." She reached over to our shard basket. "I brought you food." She pulled out a crumbly wafer for herself, exactly half of what we were given every morning. I took the wafer greedily, but slowed my chewing. We wouldn't be fed again for a long while yet.

"Where did you hide it this time?" Smuggling food or any other small object, without getting caught, was an art in Grassland. Some of the Diggers had become crafty scroungers.

"In my hair." She lifted her braids. "But I didn't even need to—there was no search this morning. The Spears all went below. I was a little scared something had happened to you."

I swallowed my first wafer. "There were a lot of Onesies

down there, Pip. More than usual. And something else, too." She looked up from the shard basket. "Threesies, maybe even Foursies were there. I saw them."

Her eyebrows lifted accusingly. "Foursies?"

I nodded. "I saw one male with *hair* on his face."

She laughed. "There could not be Foursies! They would have gone through the Separation before they came here."

"I am not lying."

Crossing her arms over her chest she chanted, "*Ones-one, twos-two . . .*"

I did the same and finished the chant for her. ". . . Spears come chasing after you."

She shook her head in disbelief. "It is true then. Did he look funny?"

I thought for a moment, recalling my brief glance at a Foursie. "No, just scared. He was big, though." I suddenly thought of Tia and Bran. "There was a female next to my cage who was probably a Threesie. She had a brother—he is about as many summers as us."

Pippa gave me a curious glance. "Did she look like a woman?"

I shrugged. "I don't know."

She nodded, then, "Was her chest bigger than mine?"

I didn't have to think about that. I nodded yes.

"How many Onesies?"

"I'm not sure . . . I'll have to think about that."

"Hmmm," she murmured. "Let's work now. I want to think for a while too. Let's fill the basket by midday so you can get some sleep and rest your shoulder."

We set to working, and despite the soreness my hands lifted the loose sand around the roots as easily as I had a thousand times before. Lift, sift, lift, sift. My fingers moved in a rhythm, sifting the dark sand with my left hand and searching for the tiny black shards with my right. Once in a while I glanced at Pippa. Since our greeting she had fallen silent, her face clouded in some brooding thought. I chatted from time to time, telling her about Tia and Bran, but she seemed far away. We filled our basket steadily and finished before the sun had reached its highest.

We walked slowly with the basket between us, watching each step for sharp stones or shells. Spilling a basket could cost us our lives. If it tipped outside of our furrow, the shards were considered anyone's property, and Diggers would run from several furrows over to steal them. By the time the Spears arrived—if they arrived—the priceless shards would be gone. Only a few days ago a boy died when his basket tipped and a stronger male beat him in order to get at the ones on the ground.

We have stumbled only once, and were lucky enough to be near smaller Diggers at the time. After I smashed the first male in the nose and blood spurted, the others backed off. But I still had to stand over the basket with my fists up while Pippa scrambled to fling the shards back in.

At the first mark we poured our basket out onto a growing mound of shards, under the watchful eye of a Spear. We held out our arms for our first brand, and the Spear made a red line just above our wrists. Brands were checked at the end of the day as we re-entered the Mouth, and anyone found without one was beaten or sent to the lower cages. Pippa said it wasn't really a brand since the marks, made from a red juice, washed off with a good scrubbing of sand and seawater. But she called them brands anyway because it made her laugh to think we were like cattle. She used to moo after we got each mark.

She didn't moo today. Instead she held my hand all the way back to the furrow without saying a word.

"What's wrong?" I asked as we sat down to lean against the thick grass stems and hide from the burning sun. We both pulled our hoods up.

She closed her eyes and pushed my legs down so that she could put her head on my lap. "Something is wrong."

"What?"

"Something is going to happen to Grassland." She was whispering, and I suddenly felt some of the fear from last night creep its way back into my stomach.

"What do you mean?"

"There have been many new Onesies coming . . . There are Threesies and Foursies in the lower cages . . . ," she muttered. "There was no search this morning, and . . . and the Spears have moved into the fields."

I lifted her head gently from my lap and stood up in the bright sun, scanning the tall grass. My eyes locked onto two Spears, standing motionless a hundred furrows away. There were four more on the opposite side, and a glint of moving metal from the direction of the caves told me that there were others—many others. I sat down again and put Pippa's head back where it had been. My legs were trembling.

"What's going on, Pippa?" My voice sounded as shaky as my legs.

"I don't know." Her tone was flat and distant, not at all like her usual self.

My heart suddenly leaped straight up through my chest. "The Spears are not going to . . . they won't . . . ?" I couldn't even say the words.

"I don't think so," she said, twisting around so that she lay on her back, looking up at me. "They would do that in the caves, not in the fields. Everyone would run if they tried to Separate us out here, and they would have to kill many. No, this is about something else."

My heart slowed just a little. "What should we do?"

"Wait. And watch even more than usual," she mumbled, drifting into an afternoon nap. I settled myself in and cradled her head so that her neck wouldn't be kinked in her sleep. But I didn't make myself too comfortable. There was an unspoken rule in Grassland that only one partner slept at a time, so that no time would be wasted for picking shards. Anything less than one and three-quarters of a basket meant a night in the lower cages. Some of the Twosies were not as strong as me, and facing a First Cleansing could be deadly. It was rare for cellmates not to reach quota.

I was a little surprised that Pippa had chosen to fall asleep. She knew that I had just been through an exhausting night, and it was not like her to be selfish when she knew I needed the rest. Perhaps she hadn't slept much last night either. I drew a deep breath and forced my eyes open, fighting the lull of the breeze and the buzzing of flies in the cool shade.

My chin hit my chest and I woke with a start. I leaped to my feet. The sun was much farther along in the sky . . . and Pippa was not there! Neither was our basket. Racing along our furrow and peering into the rows beside me, I searched for any sign of a golden head.

I located her many strides away, in the furrow beside ours, busy braiding the hair of a female about the same size as me. The thick, dark shag covering the girl's eyes couldn't hide an enormous nose that wrinkled every time Pippa teased the knots out of the long strands.

"Pippa!" I yelled. "What are you doing? There isn't

Bedford High School
Library

much time left and we still have to fill another three-quarters."

"Peace, Corki," she said. "These two made quota-full and a quarter already. They're going to give us a half for braiding her hair. You needed the sleep."

"Half," a black-haired boy croaked in a strange accent, and pointed at the basket, then at Pippa. He started jabbering in his own language, but I cut him off.

"Did he pay already?" I asked, searching for our basket.

"Yes. It's here beside me. Come and get it, and start without me. We can be finished early enough to swim." It felt good to hear her sounding happy again.

"Are you going to be all right here?"

Pippa looked up at me over a lock of hair. "I trust the girl. We have worked near her before, and she always signs Friendship. But maybe you could work the grass on the near side so you are close."

I nodded and picked up the basket. Then I turned to the boy and stuck my fist under his nose. I had seen him around before too. He was a wiry little Digger, always on the lookout for spilled baskets. "Don't touch the girl,"

I said fiercely, pointing over at Pippa. I showed a closed fist, the symbol for Death, and tapped his forehead gruffly. He understood and bowed, turning away from the girls while raising an open palm to me. Pippa caught my eye and smiled. I broke through the grass into our furrow and squatted down to the sand.

The sleep had been wonderful and I slipped into a rhythm, filling the last quarter with the thought of a swim pushing me to go faster. Some time later, as the sun ebbed in the late afternoon, Pippa came back. Between the two of us we reached our quota swiftly.

She stood up. "I need a swim, Corki."

I glanced at the sky and wiped the sand from my hands. "There is not enough time to empty the basket first. We will have to take it with us."

All of the furrows led from the mountains on the south side to the open beach at the north end. Each night the waves flooded Grassland, pouring over the tops of the stalks and rising up almost as high as the Mouth. We had seen the huge tide many times, coming toward us hungrily, when the Spears kept us out to collect more shards than usual. In the early morning the waters drew back, leaving uncountable numbers of precious shards hiding in the sand. The flooding also meant that no one could escape. Staying in Grassland past the sounding of the conch shell was the same as taking your own life.

Pippa reached the beach, then turned to me quickly. "No one is here!" she cried happily, flinging her arms in the air. I grunted, hoisting our basket just a little higher on my back. We chose a section of the beach that jutted out farther into the water. I needed a clear view of wherever we planted the basket, to stop anyone who might be hiding in the grasses from stealing it. I set it down three times before I was satisfied that our swimming spot was safe.

Pippa had already removed her clothes and was waiting for me to do the same. I looked at her, thinking of Tia, and sighed with some relief. But only some.

"What?" she said, following the direction of my eyes.

"You're getting bigger."

Her face darkened again, and I could have kicked myself for saying it.

"We'll think of something," I said.

She nodded gravely.

3

THE WATER WAS PERFECT—COLD and refreshing—after our hard work in the fields, and I felt my sweat wash away as I relaxed. We could only paddle out a little way, always with our faces to the beach. I forced myself to scan the grasses every time my head came above the water. Pippa was floating on her stomach and squirting water at me out of her mouth, all trace of seriousness gone. I splashed her back.

"You are going to wash your brand off if you keep swimming like that," I teased. I swatted at her, then did a backward flip to get away.

She stood to splash me even more, but her arms froze at her sides. "Corki, boats!"

Far out from our sandy beach three square sails were

passing the tip of the bay. We would see boats from time to time, most often at the end of the day, with their billowing orange sails full of late afternoon wind. We waved and yelled, but they disappeared, as always, around the stony arms of our bay, without even slowing down.

"Why don't they ever come here?" I splashed angrily in their direction.

When my gaze came back to the beach my eyes caught a sudden movement of the stalks fifty strides from our basket. I began a forward stroke immediately, but Pippa, in a moment of fun, had grabbed my leg. I went under, my yell cut off in a mouthful of water. I kicked—in my hurry making contact with some part of her head—and broke away. My body shot through the water like an eel's.

I broke the surface in time to see a hooded figure racing for our basket, lessening the distance to only thirty strides. With doubled energy I reached the shore, almost running before my feet even touched solid ground.

The thief dropped the shards when he saw me and made straight for the nearest furrow.

I was too quick for him. My arms clamped around his knees and I took him down by both legs into the coarse grass. We rolled over and over as he tried to squirm away. I pummeled him with punches, my arms flying wildly, my fists landing anywhere they could find flesh or bone. He got in one good kick to my head. It sent me reeling over onto my side, but I had sense enough to hold on to his foot. I flipped him off balance and came down hard on his chest, locking his head to my side with my arm. I tried squeezing his neck to cut off his air, but that only made him thrash harder. I lifted his head and threw the hood far enough back to see his face: it was the boy who had bought Pippa's braids today. Traitor. I would have to drown him.

Holding him tightly by the hair, I made him stand up with me. When we broke from the grasses Pippa stood glaring at me, an ugly red welt on the side of her face. It made her look all the more ferocious.

"Sorry!" I gasped over my shoulder as we stumbled past her. "I'll be right back."

"What are you doing?" she called after me. Pippa hated violence. When and where I could, I tried not to let her see.

"I'm taking . . . him . . . to the water!" The boy began

thrashing crazily, knowing he was about to die. I raised my fist to punch him.

"Corki, no! I'll send myself to the lower cages if you do anything else to him."

I threw the punch wide. I tried to look back at Pippa, to beg for her understanding, and the boy punched me. I howled in pain. He bolted for the furrows, running like a sparrow from a hundred hawks.

I felt Pippa's hand on my head. "Are you hurt?"

"Guess," I gasped. Experience in the grasses had taught me to deal with my enemies even when they had run away. I forced myself to turn toward the furrows.

"Are you bleeding?" she asked.

I ignored the question. "What did you do *that* for? He's going to try and steal from us again now. He might even tell others. My fist will mean nothing."

She stroked my head. "But you mustn't kill, Corki. It is a very bad thing."

"Why? He tried to take our quota even after you made them a braid."

"It still isn't right."

Pippa was so hard to understand sometimes. She didn't

act like the others, and even when she made me so angry I wanted dump a bucket of shards on her, I always gave in to her quiet ways. I straightened, to get my breath back while she picked up our work-cloths. I had to wash in the water to get rid of the sand. Before I dressed, Pippa looked me over to make sure there was no blood anywhere.

By the time the conch shell blew she had me laughing, swinging her one free arm while we carried the basket, pretending to be me fighting with the thief. I apologized again for kicking her. When our basket was empty we received our second brand and joined the long line of tired Diggers at the end of the furrows, to begin the slow march back to the caves of the Twosies.

"Look." Pippa pointed out to the sea. The sun was setting for the day, sending brilliant red flames across the sky and turning the fields of Grassland into red-gold. I gave a halfhearted glance and continued to search the line of Twosies for the thief.

At the Mouth we handed in our work-cloths and followed the Spears to the Neck for our evening Cleansing. The long tunnel was lit only by faint light that reached from the Mouth to the inner cells. The Spears at the front and back waited until every last Digger was positioned along the Neck, then stood back to avoid the shower of water from above. Pippa always looked forward to the Cleansing, even after a swim.

"Don't you feel so good after the Cleansing?" she said.

"I feel wet," I muttered, letting the gentle streams soak my aching shoulder.

"I don't know what I'd do without it." Her face was turned upward so that the water splashed over her eyes and mouth.

"You're crazy, Pippa." I laughed.

"Coriko!" a voice called from somewhere down the line.

I froze. Pippa choked.

"Coriko!" It was Bran.

"Shut up!" I yelled back. No one was ever sure if the Spears knew our names, and I wasn't willing to find out.

"Good to hear you!" he said once again.

"You too!" I hissed.

Pippa gave me a slap on the shoulder. "Don't. No more nights in the cages."

I fell silent, absolutely shocked that Bran was in the Twosies' line. Was Tia with him?

When the water stopped we received our cell-wraps and prepared to be locked in for the night. A Spear gave a halfhearted tug at both our braids before pushing us into our home.

"What was *that*?" I whispered. "He didn't check for anything. I could have brought in a fistful of shells and he wouldn't have known." Pippa was right—as usual. Something really strange was going on.

"They are nervous." Pippa's eyes were thoughtful as she watched the Spears march to the end of the passage, then vanish into darkness. "I can feel it."

"And what is a Onesie doing in a Twosie line, Pip?"

"I . . . don't know. I've never seen it happen before. It wasn't good for him to call out your name, though. And *you* should have known better than to answer back. We were lucky he didn't hear us earlier when we were outside the Mouth."

"Are you saying *you* wouldn't have said anything if he had called your name?"

She took my hand, pulled me to the back of our cell,

and sat me down so that we faced each other cross-legged on the cool ground. I kissed my palm, touched the wall and said, "This is a place of peace." Pippa did the same. We never argued at the wall. It was our place to talk, to forgive, and to think. Pippa prayed there every night.

She still hadn't let go of my hand. "After the Feeding, when the torches go out, we will have a long talk. You must tell me everything that happened with the boy and girl. Everything. You can have some time to think while we eat, but then you must remember the smallest to the greatest of things that happened."

"I can do that."

She lifted up her palm to me. "I'm sorry I got mad during the Cleansing," she said quietly. "I just don't ever want to spend a night alone again. I have nothing but you, Corki, and strange things are happening." I raised my hand and our fingers interlocked.

The clang of opening gates caused us to sit up. We stood, kissed the wall, then walked toward the front of the cell. Spears were coming, carrying sacks of dried fish and wafers and tossing the food toward the outstretched arms of the Diggers. I could catch better than Pippa, so I stood in the center of the bars where the Spears usually aimed and prepared to snatch.

What I caught in the end was one strip of dried fish and a soggy wafer that started to break apart in my fingers. I stared at the Spear, expecting him to throw again, but the masked face moved on to the next cell.

"Pippa? What is going on?" We had never received this little before, not even when I missed a catch.

She gave a gasp and wiped at her eyes. "It's all right, Corki. We'll . . . be fine."

We ate in silence. While I tried to think of all the details from last night, I listened to the sounds of grumbling as the Diggers all yammered complaints in their own languages. Pippa made me eat most of the fish.

"I'll have something from the beach tomorrow," she tried, smiling.

When our meager meal was over, we waited until the torches were out before we started talking. Normally after the Feeding we played thinking games or drew pictures in the soft dirt of the floor. Her favorite thing to draw was trees and I got to know the skinny, sticklike branches very well. She managed to hide at least one in everything she made.

We also practiced my writing. Pippa would hold my hand in hers and draw letters on the dirt floor, tracing the symbols over and over until I could perform them without her control. In the morning when the Spears came by with torches and, briefly, we could see, I would make the symbols again and Pippa would nod her approval. She had come to Grassland knowing a lot of language, more than most Northerners I had seen so far, and she was slowly teaching me everything she could remember. But tonight, with the tense mood in the caves and the strange events of the past day, we lay down on our mat of sweet grasses, side by side, to talk.

"Tell me what you remember," she whispered.

"Everything started off normal," I began. "They were packed in their cages as usual, except that it sounded like there were more than two in some of the cages. It definitely smelled like more."

"How many Spears?"

"There were two every six cages, all the way down—"

"Any more?"

I thought again. "Yes. The ones with the red mark—there were more of them than usual. But most of them didn't come in. They stayed out by the entrance."

Someone was relieving himself in a nearby cell, and the smell broke into our conversation.

"Put some grass on it, idiot!" I yelled. The offender hooted, and when a second waft of stink blew past us there were moans and giggles all over. But even that didn't spoil my time with Pippa. It felt so good to be lying beside her again in the warmth of our private cell, with our familiar walls and no metal bars at the sides.

Pippa leaned over and touched her nose to my shoulder. "Did anything smell different?"

I pictured the cages. "There was more sweat."

"Hmmm." She pulled away. "So there were many older ones, not just a few." I could hear her hand slapping the ground, a habit she couldn't stop even when she was thinking in her sleep. "More Spears . . . Threesies and Foursies . . ." Her tapping got louder.

"Why didn't they give us very much food?" I asked.

"Hmmm. I think they are saving it for some reason . . . Maybe to feed all the new ones."

"Then I hate the new ones. I am still hungry."

"Tell me about Tia and Bran." Pippa's tapping stopped and she leaned her head onto my chest. "Tell me what they looked like and smelled like. And how Tia is like a woman."

I remembered Tia's terrified face as the Spears entered their cage, and her strong voice even after the waters came. "She is tall—"

"How tall?"

"Are you going to let me tell?"

"Don't forget anything."

"She is tall—at least one hand more than me."

"That's pretty tall."

"Yes. And they both have blackish-brown hair. Bran's hair is short, no braids. Tia's is long, but she doesn't have braids either."

"She will learn quickly," Pippa said. "She is a woman. She can do lots of things."

I thought of the First Cleansing. "She is strong, too. She held Bran against the bars and they both lived. And when a Spear hit Tia, Bran went to kick, but I yelled at him and he stopped. They are smart." I explained to her everything I could remember, but she still had more questions.

"What did her face look like?"

"Her face is like her. Strong, scared, but wanting to live."

"What about their clothes? Did she look nice in her clothes?"

"That is a silly question, Pippa. I don't know. They were clothes. They fell away from her like everyone's do."

"Yes, but what did the clothes *look* like?"

I sighed. "I don't know the word, but the top of her garment had . . . spaces . . . like when we lock our fingers."

"Like dry seaweed on the rocks?"

"A little bit like that, but the patterns all made sense."

She sat up. "I think I remember something like that."

"You do?"

"Yes. I can almost picture it."

We were quiet for a while. I tried to figure out why Pippa was asking so many questions about Tia, but before I opened my mouth she gave me part of an answer.

"I would like to wear woman clothes someday," she said dreamily.

"No, you don't."

She lay back down. "One day we will leave Grassland,

Corki. Together. And then I will wear woman clothes and we will live by beautiful trees."

"What will I wear?" I asked.

"Man clothes." I could hear her smile. I turned on my side toward her and leaned on my elbow.

"What do you think is happening, Pip?"

Her hand started tapping again. "I think the Spears are afraid."

"What could Spears be afraid of?"

Her tapping stopped. "*That's* what makes me afraid."

She put her head back on my chest and began to sing quietly, like she did every night before we fell asleep. Then her breathing became more regular and I felt my own eyelids close, bounce open, then close again.

Muffled waves pounding their constant rhythms against the lip of the Mouth made endless echoes in the rocky cells. Pippa suddenly gripped me tighter in a dream, and I heard her mumble, "I *will* be a woman." All night long my own dreams were filled with terror, as visions of Tia screaming, and Pippa being torn from my arms, made me tremble.

4

TWO BASKETS?" I STARED QUESTIONingly at Pippa and rubbed the spot on my chest where the Spear had pushed the containers into me. She flipped her hood over her head and stepped away from the first mark into the sunlight.

"No. They want four," she said dully.

"Four? They want *four*? How can we do four? We can't. It's too much."

"Then we will be getting a beating tonight." She marched purposefully toward our furrow, trying not to trip over the extra-large garment she had been given. The Spears never bothered about proper sizes.

"Pippa, this is crazy." I jogged to catch up to her, looking around me to see how the other Twosies were dealing with the news. There was general confusion everywhere as hand signals were flying and a buzz whispered over the grasses.

She dropped to her knees and began working immediately, thrusting her hands into the moist sand before I had even gotten there.

"Something is making the Spears afraid, Corki. Something is making them do things differently in Grassland."

"What could it be?" I began sifting. When she didn't answer, I said, "Maybe they stole too many Onesies this time and they have to put us all together. That's why Bran was in our line."

"Maybe," she said. But she didn't seem convinced.

Often in the mornings as the shadow disappeared back into the mountains, Pippa would sing while we worked. She would make up songs with silly words about Spears who had no heads, or flying shards that danced in the moonlight above an ocean-covered Grassland. Other times she would sing about Outside, about trees and animals and things I didn't really know about or remember. But today there were no songs, only gusty breaths as she tried to keep up with my pace. Lift and sift . . . lift and sift.

Soon sweat was pouring down to splash on the upturned earth in front of me. I threw back my hood even though the sun was just entering its full heat.

"We need some water," Pippa croaked.

I nodded, sitting back on my haunches. My fingers ached, and we had only filled the basket halfway. We stood slowly, and as I gripped the handles to lift our shards a long shadow ran across my foot. I dropped the basket, swung around and raised my fists. The sun blinded us as we turned. I pushed Pippa behind me with one arm, ready for the first strike of a fist.

But none came.

"Coriko?"

"Tia?" I shaded my eyes with a hand and stepped forward. Pippa didn't move.

The grasses rustled and Tia stepped forward into our furrow, followed by Bran.

"What are you doing here?" I lowered my fists slowly.

Bran removed his hood, revealing bloodshot eyes and a haggard face. "They sent us out here today. We don't know where to work. No one tells us what to do. Every time we choose a spot and start working we get attacked. We have come from way back there." He pointed far behind him.

They both looked exhausted, and from the tearstains on his face I guessed that he had been crying already this morning. Pippa moved forward and clutched the back of my work-cloth.

"You can work here," I said. "There is plenty. We don't know what's going on either, but you are welcome with us. We will not steal any of your work."

"Thank you, Coriko." Tia smiled. She sounded tired as well. "And you must be Pippa?"

When I turned to my side I found that Pippa had disappeared behind me, wrapping her arms about my waist and burying her face into my back.

"Pippa," I scolded. "Come out. What are you doing?"

Tia laughed gently. "She's shy."

"Pippa!" I pulled her interlocked hands apart and dragged her in front of me. Her face was all red and she kept looking at me instead of the others. I scowled at her.

Tia took a step forward. "You are even more beautiful than Coriko said you were, Pippa," she said.

I didn't remember saying anything like that. But Pippa was already turning to face our tall guest. Her face blossomed into a smile.

Tia reached out a hand. "Would you show me how to work? We don't know what we are doing, and I could use another woman's advice."

I sputtered at the word "woman," but when Pippa shot me an angry glance I sobered and pointed at the basket. "Only cellmates work together." There was a moment of silence.

"I will work with Tia," Pippa announced, taking the tall girl's hand and leading her down the furrow.

Bran looked at me and I shrugged. "Everything's changing." I picked up their basket and began the task of teaching him how to lift and sift. It felt strange to work beside a boy when all my life I had been with Pippa. Bran was a fast learner and he had energy. I glanced at him from time to time, admiring his speed, although I was forced to shut my eyes when his reckless hands flung sand in my direction. At least the Onesies were still only required to fill one basket each. I had no idea how we would have filled eight.

"How long have you been here?" he gasped as he worked.

"What do you mean?"

"How long have you been a slave?"

A slave. I had to sort out his words in my head. "Eight or nine summers."

"Did they attack your village?"

I tried to make a picture word for village. "The Spears brought me to Grassland over a lot of sand—that is all I remember. The rest has been lost. Pippa remembers more. She sings about it once in a while."

"Is she your sister?" Although his hands never stopped moving, he glanced up at me.

"No."

He wiped at his sweaty forehead. "Well, do you have anyone else here? Any brothers or sisters who came with you?"

"There is no one else here who speaks our language. There was one Threesie, a few summers ago—we called him White Eye because of his odd eyebrow—but he is gone now. So there is only Pippa. And now you. Shut up and work, Bran."

We worked in silence then, filling the basket as the shadow of the mountains continued its slow disappearance. Once in a while I heard giggles coming from Pippa and Tia, and a strange feeling began forming in my chest. It bothered me like a fly in the face. I found myself working harder every time I heard them.

"Full," Bran said with a sigh a while later.

"That was fast." I smiled at the brimming basket. "Let's go see how they are doing." He nodded and wiped his dirty hands on his work-cloth. I tugged on Pippa's braid as we approached, and they stopped talking.

"We have filled one," I said triumphantly.

Tia looked inside their basket. "So have we—almost." At the first mark we handed in our shards and received our brands. Pippa took my hand on the way back to the furrow and I felt a warm shiver of comfort shoot through me at her touch.

"I like Tia," she whispered.

"Is she a good worker?" I whispered back.

"Of course."

I narrowed my eyes. "Don't giggle and talk so much when we go back, or we won't reach quota."

She nodded. "You know we are going to make it. It just means we don't get to swim. And we are going to be very tired tonight." She was right, of course, even if Bran and Tia were to leave us at this point we still would be able to finish.

"What were you laughing about, you two? All the time laughing and giggling."

She brought her other hand up to her mouth, broke into giggles, and looked away from me.

"What?" I asked, pulling my hand away from her.

"Woman things," she whispered, and skipped ahead to catch up to Tia.

By midday we had returned from the mark with two more empty baskets and we lay low in the grasses to rest. Tia removed her hood and Pippa began braiding her long dark hair. In my memory I had never had a conversation with this many people before, and I found myself getting confused when two or more talked at the same time.

"Your hair is so nice," Pippa was saying.

"I can't wait till you've finished." Tia touched the top of her head. "You and Coriko have such beautiful braids."

"When it gets longer, it will be even prettier." Pippa

examined the shorter strands. Tia was looking much more relaxed than she had this morning, and I smiled at her closed eyes.

Bran had a scowl on his face, flicking pebbles at a large stalk in front of him. I had been watching him throughout the day and it was becoming obvious that something was troubling him.

"When are we going to get out of here?" he asked suddenly.

Pippa stopped working. We stared at him.

"When are we going to *escape*?"

I got up to my knees and looked around, taking note of the nearest Spears. But they stood silently in their long dark cloaks, their masked faces never ceasing to search the grasses. When I settled back down I said in a quiet voice, "There are certain words that the Spears seem to understand in any language. That is one of them."

Bran's face went white and he sat up himself to look around.

"No one," I said, "*no* one . . . gets to Outside. Runaways are killed or come floating back with the tide. And the Spears guard the caves."

"Who *are* they?" Tia asked softly.

I looked at Pippa and shrugged. She flipped one of Tia's new braids and pinned it with a finger. "They watch us."

"What tribe are they from?"

We didn't know what to say. Spears were Spears.

Tia crinkled her forehead. "Do they speak? What language do they have?"

Again I shrugged. "We have never heard a Spear. They do not speak to us or to each other. They watch and they punish."

She nodded, then muttered, "They were sure in a hurry to get us into the mountain. It felt like they were being chased."

I couldn't imagine anything being able to chase a Spear.

"And no wonder," she continued. "There are children from many lands here. There must be a lot of angry people up and down the coasts and across the seas, wanting their own kind back."

"I have a memory," Pippa said. "Of a night when we first journeyed across the sands to Grassland. The Spears who brought us all wore the red fist on their chests." She traced a spot below her throat. "I have seen them other times since . . . but always in the caves, never in the fields. They let my sister fall away from the chain line because her foot was cut and she couldn't walk properly. They left her behind like an empty shell . . . I think about her at night." She paused. "Somewhere in the desert we met up with a group of white-cloaked men who led a line of slaves. The Spears traded all but three of us from our village. The white-cloaked men seemed to want yellow-haired people. They kept grabbing at our heads. The Spears wanted a mix—I think they didn't like anyone talking to each other on the way. When we finally reached Grassland, I was the only one from my village who survived the desert heat."

"How terrible," Tia murmured. "You must have been terrified."

"Yes. But then I met Corki." She gave me a big smile and I could feel my cheeks turning red.

"How did you two become . . . mates?" Bran asked.

"I was crying for my sister as we all stood in the Hollow—"

"The what?" Bran asked.

"It is the way in—the opening to Grassland from the desert. I have only seen it once, when I came here. It was guarded by more Spears than I could count."

Bran nodded.

"There was darkness and crying everywhere. The Spears lit torches and in the light I suddenly saw many cages with children inside lying on the grasses. I was pushed into one that had a very brave, blond-haired boy sitting at the back, staring at me."

"Coriko!" Bran said, perking up.

I smiled. "You were so little."

She crinkled her nose. "So were you. Corki helped me live through the First Cleansing, and we haven't been apart since then. Except for the times when he gets himself in trouble." She glared at me.

Tia touched Pippa's cheek. "You must miss your family so much."

"I think of them sometimes. But they are disappearing in my mind. I can't remember my mother's face anymore."

"Do you think they are still alive?"

"I think so. I would like to think they are. My sister and I were taken from the fields where we were playing, so

I don't know what happened to everyone else. There were some other children I knew who were also taken, but they were traded too."

Tia felt the back of her head to touch Pippa's work. "We were taken from the fields as well. By the time I saw their black helmets breaking from the trees toward us it was too late. What about you, Coriko?"

I stared at the roots of the stalks until Pippa spoke up. "He doesn't remember much. We have tried but . . . he just can't." I stole a peek at Tia, then turned quickly when I realized that she was watching me.

"I don't have a family," I said. "I already told Bran. I just have Pippa."

Tia nodded silently, then shifted her position. "What are the shards for?"

I shook my head in disbelief. So many questions these Threesies asked. "I think they eat them," I said. Pippa laughed.

"They are metal of some kind, I think," Tia said slowly, holding one up to her eye. "Or at least a very light rock that has metal in it." She flicked the shard high into the next furrow. "Maybe they use them for weapons." She turned to look at Pippa. "Where do they go? I mean, where do they take the shards?"

"I have wondered about that before," Pippa said, to my surprise. "My guess is, Outside." She said the last word quietly.

"Then that is where we have to go." Bran leaned forward.

"This is silly talk," I said, standing up. "Family and Outside. Who cares? We have shards to pick. Talking about nothing doesn't fill the basket."

"It's not nothing, Coriko." Tia tugged gently away from Pippa. "Bran is right. We may not be allowed to say the word, but I am going to think it, until the four of us are back where we belong. Don't you ever think about that?"

"No!" I said. I picked up an empty basket and walked down the furrow, kicking at loose stones along the way. But I had not told the truth. Every summer Pippa was beginning to look more like a Threesie, and I wasn't far behind myself. We had promised each other that we would never be apart. We spent many hours thinking about how we could avoid the Separation. But no good plans had come. Only Outside was there hope of us being together.

Left to my angry thoughts, I fumed while I sifted, pouring more and more shards into the basket. Pippa worked beside me toward the end of the day, and although she didn't say anything, I knew she had also taken Tia's words to heart.

At the last conch blast we emptied our baskets onto the pile and joined the weary line of Diggers. I was too tired to be angry anymore, especially when Pippa leaned her head against my shoulder. Bran stumbled several times as we shuffled in the sand. When we passed the mark I was surprised again to find that there were no Spears standing in their usual positions. I swung my head around and found them in a long line, facing us, their prods pointed in our direction. And then I noticed something else.

"Pippa"—I nudged her off my shoulder—"what are *they* carrying?"

She looked up and stared in the direction of my pointing finger. A number of Spears with the red fist on their chests were waiting in the sun. Strange, curved sticks were attached to their backs. A few of those closest to us were actually holding the sticks in their hands.

"Bow and arrow," Tia whispered back at us. "You use the curved part to shoot the short stick."

"Why would they have those?" I asked. "And why have the red-fist Spears come out of the mountain?"

Pippa was wide-awake now. Her eyes immediately went up toward the mountains, and she followed the half circle of our closed bay, searching the stony ridges above us. Then she looked down at the sand. "I think I know why there are so many changes in Grassland," she whispered.

"Why?"

Her voice was hollow. "They are preparing for war."

A chill ran down my back, and Tia whipped her head around to stare at Pippa with wide eyes. She turned her gaze up toward the mountains as well. When her eyes met mine she nodded slowly, gravely, then stepped forward as the line trudged into the shadow of the caves.

5

"AND BLESS GRASSLAND," PIPPA whispered fervently.

"And bless Grassland," I mumbled. We unfolded our hands, kissed the wall, then shuffled over to our bed of hay and sweet grasses. I was so tired I slept through Pippa's entire prayer, but at least I woke when she reached the end. I waited for her to wrap her arm around my stomach before we fell asleep. A slurping sound made me lift my head, and I reached back with one hand until I found her face. "Are you sucking your thumb?" I asked.

"Am mhot."

"Yes you are! You haven't done that for a long time. What are you worried about?"

"Muphing."

"Pippa." The slurping stopped. "Are you scared about war?"

"Yes." I could feel her shivering.

"What else?"

Pause. "Bad things are going to happen, Corki." Her voice was so tiny in the blackness.

"No, they're not." I pulled her thumb gently away from her mouth, wrapped her arm around me like a blanket, and held on to her hand. "Go to sleep, Pippa. I will take care of you. I always have."

"Even the Spears are scared," she whispered.

I was so tired, I couldn't have cared if an army of Spears decided to whack their prods against the bars of our cell all night long.

"We have been asleep too long, Corki. Grassland has been asleep. The Outside has come to us and we need to be ready."

"I will take care of you, Pippa," I mumbled, not really knowing what she was talking about.

"What about Tia and Bran?"

"They will be well too."

"Promise?"

"Hmmm." Sometime later I hardly noticed her arm pulling away from me. I fell asleep to the sound of slurping.

Grassland awakened the next day, as it always had, and before the early morning shadows had moved fifty strides closer to the eastern mountains, the four of us were hard at work in the fields. But for all the sameness of the sun and sky, there was a brooding apprehension blowing from the hills. Despite my words of comfort to Pippa I could feel the tension in the air and, without even discussing it, the four of us worked within touching distance, side by side.

Pippa was exhausted already, and if I guessed correctly, she hadn't slept much last night. Tia also looked worn, saying only a few words as she sifted the sand beside me. Bran attacked the sand as he had the day before, and if he felt any fear he was hiding it well.

"This sure beats cleaning chickens," he puffed cheerfully, wiping sweat from his matted forehead.

"What are chickens?" I asked.

He gave me a puzzled look. "They are white birds.

Well . . . some are speckled or brown. They are about this big." He opened his hands a little more than two palms wide. "They don't fly. They have small pointed beaks. And we eat them!" He flapped his arms and made squawking noises. He looked very silly and I laughed at him, wondering why anyone would be crazy enough to eat a bird. Fish was tasty, but *birds*? They had feathers.

At midday there was another change. When we received our brands, we were only handed back two baskets.

"Only one more each?" Tia asked.

Pippa looked concerned and raised her head to the mountains like she had yesterday.

"We can go swimming," I suggested. Bran was excited immediately, but Pippa remained silent the entire walk back to the furrow. When our baskets were filled I stretched my back, still feeling the pains from yesterday. "Let's go to the beach."

Again Pippa looked around us. "I don't think we should, Corki."

"Come on, Pippa. There are four of us now. We can actually play while one person watches the baskets."

Pippa's eyebrows shot up and a smile slowly edged over

her lips. I didn't hesitate. I jumped up, grabbed one end of a basket, and began dragging it down the furrow toward the shoreline. Bran followed, picking up the other end and hooting as we went.

When we reached the beach there were several other Diggers already in the water. They paddled quickly to shore the moment they saw us. We stayed close together, looking for a quiet place to put our baskets down.

"I will guard them," Tia said. She looked uncomfortably at the naked Diggers running on the beach, then back at us. Pippa and I removed our clothes and flung them down on top of the shards. Bran stood staring at Pippa, a redness beginning to creep from his neck to his forehead.

"I—I—we . . ." He glanced at his sister for help, but she was also turning red.

Pippa came to their rescue. "Do you not know how to swim, Bran?"

I should have thought of it myself. Of course, they were embarrassed.

But he shook his head. "No, I can swim. It's just that . . ." He looked again at his sister.

"We are not used to being naked," Tia blurted out.

They were very silly, these two.

"Why don't you wear your cloths in the water?" Pippa suggested. "We have finished work, so you no longer need them dry."

Tia smiled appreciatively. "I really would like to swim."

"I can put mine back on if it helps," Pippa offered. I showed Pippa two fingers. *Shut up*. I couldn't bear the idea of swimming with a clumsy cloth getting all caught and twisted around my legs. She signed *Peace* back to me and nodded toward our cloths in the basket.

Grumbling, I slipped back into the work-cloth. Bran's face remained red and he giggled as Pippa put her cloth back on. I whacked the back of his head. "Don't be such a Onesie."

The water cured all of our worries. Bran and I wrestled, playfully trying to outdo each other as we splashed about. Pippa floated, occasionally kicking at me or mounting my shoulders so I could throw her backward into the water. It felt so wonderful to know I could play while a big Threesie stood guard over our basket, that I actually stopped searching the beach. Sometime later I turned to look for

Pippa and found the dark face of Tia coming straight at me. Before I could pull back she gave a laugh and pushed my head underwater with amazing force. I felt Bran shoot past me as I came to the surface and watched him tackle his sister, taking her down with him. Pippa waved from the beach.

We floated for a while, letting the waves roll us in toward the shore.

"I haven't felt this good in so long!" Bran yelled to the sky. Tia had a grin on her face that wouldn't come off. I felt strong and wild and happy all at the same time as the water washed my worries of war and change into the ocean. And best of all, as their faces kept telling me, each one of us was feeling the same thing.

"Your turn, Pippa!" I called, paddling for the beach. She was sitting with the basket between her legs, following my approach with a hand up to shade her eyes from the brilliant reflection off the water. She stood when I shook my soaking hair at her but did not appear to be annoyed with me in the slightest.

"They are nice, aren't they?"

"Yes. I like them. Bran is fun to play with."

"Sit down." Her face was calm and she folded her hands. "Do you think I look like Tia?"

I shook my head. "No. Tia has dark hair and yours is as bright as the sun. Sometimes it hurts my eyes to look at you in the fields."

She smiled. "Yes, but do I look like her—like a woman, I mean?"

I groaned. "Why do you keep talking about that?"

"Because I want to look like a woman. I want to *be* a woman. I want to look like Tia. She is so pretty, and strong, and . . ."

I picked up a handful of sand and threw it into the water. "I don't want you to be a woman, and *I* don't want to become a Threesie, either. They will Separate us."

"You promised we would never be apart again. And they didn't Separate Tia."

I reached for another handful of sand. "That is because of the strange things that we don't know about. But it will go away—and so will Tia when everything is normal again. You know that, Pippa."

"Do you *want* her to go away?" she said.

"No! Of course I don't. I like them both. But when

the Spears stop coming out into the sun and more food is given to us, then the Separation will come, and she *will* go. That is the way it has always been."

She lifted a shard from the top of the basket and placed it in her palm. She jiggled it, gently allowing it to work its way to the edge. Then slowly she turned her hand over to let the shiny shard drop down to the hundreds of others waiting below. "I don't want Tia to go and I still want to be a woman," she said, so quietly I could barely hear her.

"Why do you want something that will Separate us?"

"You promised we would never be Separated," she fired back.

I was silent, my grim mood rapidly returning.

"Coriko, you promised me."

"Yes, I did." My feelings of fun were disappearing into the air like a small pool of water in the hot sun. Ever since Tia had arrived, Pippa had been stuck on the idea of being a woman—a thing that made me more frightened than anything else. "And if you don't want us to be Separated, then you had better start praying harder." I wiped at the tears beginning to form, desperately hoping no one around could see.

"I will," she said, brushing her hand over my cheek. "And—" Her words were suddenly cut off by the sound of the conch shell being blown. *Now?* We hadn't expected to hear that sound for a long while yet.

The conch shell wailed again, blowing its urgency toward us and making our hearts leap into our mouths. All down the beach the Diggers froze. Some in the water, others on the sand, all sitting up straight and listening as if it were the only sound the mighty ocean had to give us.

I turned to call Bran and Tia, but Pippa had already leaped to her feet, screaming as she ran. I hooked an arm through a handle of the basket and waited impatiently until Bran charged up to grip the other side.

"What's going on?" he said breathlessly.

"I don't—"

My heartbeat tripled again as screams broke out on the beach a short way down from us. We both turned to look. Spears were breaking through the grasses, their long prods aimed low, with the sharp wicked ends pointed to the ocean. Their black robes and boots kicked up the sand as they marched forward onto the beach.

"Run!" I yelled, letting go of the basket and turning to grab Pippa's hand.

Bran continued to hold the other end. "What is hap—?"

"Run, you stupid Onesie!" I yelled again. "Run for the caves."

Tia was white-faced as she stared at the Diggers running crazily off the beach. I grabbed her hand as well to shake her from her fear.

"This way, Bran," Pippa called out as he started in the wrong direction. A Spear suddenly pushed through the grasses in front of us, only a few paces away from Bran, his dark mask showing nothing but danger. His flashing weapon cut the heads off the last stalks as he emerged and I pulled hard on the girls' hands to steer them toward the furrows on our left. I hoped that Bran had the sense to follow. From the corner of my eye I saw him throw himself to the side to avoid the Spear, then scramble in somewhere behind us.

We burst through the long golden stems and ran like the wind, not looking back and desperately trying not to fall in the uneven furrows. The stones and the fallen shards from baskets cut into my feet. Several times I would have tumbled if Tia's strong hand hadn't held me steady. Spears were everywhere, chasing Diggers toward the caves like a herd of ants toward a hill.

"Is Bran with us?" I called over my shoulder.

"I'm beside you!"

I allowed myself a fast glance through the stalks on our left and saw his broken shadow racing beside us.

"Pippa?" I yelled. "What is all this?"

"Don't know! Keep running!"

When we reached the first mark a mass of swarming Diggers forced us to slow down, and I took a moment to look around. Everyone was yelling, trying to find cellmates and avoid the Spears who pushed and kicked us toward the Mouth.

"They are herding us to the caves." Tia dropped my hand.

"Why are they making us go in this early?" I asked, pushing aside a Digger who came too close.

Pippa lifted her head and searched the tops of the cliffs. Never taking her eyes off the mountains she said, "The Outside has come."

The Spears formed a line again as we, along with the other Diggers, were pressed into a squirming wedge against the rock. The bottoms of my feet hurt terribly. When I looked down I saw blood oozing out from between my toes.

A shadow suddenly fell over us and I looked up to see what it was. A drifting darkness, like a cloud moving swiftly over the mountain, had formed above our heads. I gasped at its strange appearance. It looked like a thousand birds arching upward. Then it dropped sharply and fell toward us.

"Oh save us," Tia whimpered beside me. "Those are arrows." She grabbed at Bran and threw him to the ground. He looked as if he were about to faint.

The cloud descended with remarkable speed, and by the time Tia's words had made it to my head, Pippa was already pulling me down with her.

There was a noise like many stones thudding into the sand at the same time. I saw Diggers fall to the ground as we had. Screaming broke out everywhere. A foot went into my stomach as the Diggers around us began to break the line and run back out toward the furrows. I stood, quickly raising Pippa with me so we would not be trampled. On my way up a Digger fell against me and I rolled him off my shoulder onto the ground. A stick about the size of a grass stalk—what Tia had called an arrow—was poking out of his chest. He lay on his back where I had dropped him, without a single sound.

Pippa's face was filled with horror. I stood frozen, staring at the dead Digger. A second shadow appeared and we all looked up.

"Run to the furrows!" Tia yelled. "Run, run, run!"

The pain in my feet was gone. All I could think of was to hide from the death cloud, to flee as far away from the mountain as I could.

The sound of the arrows thumping into the ground behind us made me move faster than I ever have before in my life. They came like rain as we raced across the grasses, louder as they rushed toward us. Then something struck my leg with a searing pain and I fell face-first into the sand.

Another shadow came over me, but this time even in my pain I knew it wasn't the death cloud. I looked up and the light above began to spin, the mountains becoming a swirling darkness in the afternoon sky.

"Corki!" a voice yelled from somewhere nearby.

I felt hands on my shoulders, turning me, and saw Pippa's face, her beautiful face, all tearstained, all white, calling my name. Grassland stopped swirling. Bran and Tia stood over me too, panting and frightened.

"Pippa!" I gasped.

"It is in your leg!" she wailed.

I tried to sit up, but the swirling took me and I felt ready to retch.

"We have to get him up," I heard Tia say, "and back to the Mouth now. We're too exposed out here. The caves are the only place to hide."

When I lay still the pain was much worse, but at least the earth and sky were where they were supposed to be. Tears streamed down my cheeks and when I tried to speak only garble came out. Fear gripped me. I couldn't stop my body from shaking. All I wanted was to get up and run.

Voices and faces blurred above me. "Tia." Pippa's trembling voice. "We need to cover the wound." Then Tia's voice. "I'll take the cloth from that one over there." I felt my leg being lifted.

And then the cloud of arrows came again, filling the sky once more as if to hide the sun. For the briefest moment my head cleared. "Go, Pippa!" I gasped. "Go."

She threw herself on my chest, sobbing.

"Get her off, Bran. Make her run."

Hands ripped my Pippa away from me, and as they ran with her between them I heard her sob, "You promised . . . You *promised*!"

"Run," I croaked.

Lying on my back, I had a perfect view of the arrows as they made their final arc toward me. When they struck this time, the sound of them hitting the ground came from behind me, toward the ocean. I listened, my fingers gritted into the sand, for their final strike.

"I love you, Pippa," I whispered.

6

I OPENED MY EYES. THE ARROWS had landed beyond me. The few I could see poking out of the grass must have come from the second attack. I waited for a long time for the next dark cloud of arrows, but the blue sky remained clear, as if Outside had finished with us for the moment.

The screaming of other Diggers grew faint—unlike the throbbing in my leg, which seemed to grow with every breath I took. The pain brought me wave after wave of retching and dizziness until I thought I could be sick no more. I do not know how long I lay there. When my eyes opened again the sun was dropping behind the ridge of rock that jutted out from the beach—a giant golden ball saying good night to an awakened Grassland.

"Where are you going?" I whispered. "We are awake now. Will you leave us in darkness too?"

The ocean was louder now. A chilly wind blew across the top of my body, bringing with it the salt smell of the sea. The cold helped my thoughts focus, and despite the raging fire in my leg I pushed with my still-clenched fists to sit up. In the setting rays of light I saw Grassland deserted, a sight I had never seen before. The caves, large black holes in the distance, looked far away—though on a normal day I could have reached them in three hundred strides.

I looked down at my wound. At first I couldn't see anything, because someone had tried to tie a cloth around my leg to stop the bleeding. "Pippa," I murmured. Fresh tears rose to my eyes. I eased the cloth back from the wound. Mistake. The sharp end of the arrow was poking out through the top of my thigh. I retched again and the dizziness returned so strongly I fainted.

Sometime later I felt water touching the back of my head. I sat up quickly. The last rays of sun blinded me across a bright glass of sea that had found its way to me. Grassland was flooding.

My blood pounded, and fear gripped me stronger than the pain. Using only my left leg I worked my way up to my knee, keeping my injured leg out straight like a prod. If only I had something to hold on to. But there was no time for wishing. Already water swirled over the tops of my toes.

The journey to the caves looked about as far as the horizon did. With each step I wept, gritting my teeth and counting, singing, cursing—anything to drown out the pain.

I had made about twenty strides when I came across my first body. I had seen many deaths before. Some of them had been unpleasant, but this was different—this came from Outside. It was a boy lying twisted in the grasses with his face away from me. I was glad I couldn't see his eyes. There were other bodies around, but none showed any sign of life. I passed them as if they were shards ready to be taken by the sea when it reached them.

I took a rest after about forty strides. When I turned to check on the ocean's progress a groan erupted at my feet, louder than the whistling wind through the stalks. I looked down and to my left. Another boy lay in the fading light, his face upturned to me and one arm reaching out for help.

I stared briefly into his dark eyes. It was the thief.

"Thief!" I hissed, wasting a breath on him. I decided to rest elsewhere and was about to move on when he groaned again and turned his hand into a downturned fist. *Mercy.*

"Mercy?" I spat. I took a hop forward in the direction of the caves. Again he groaned.

Pippa . . .

I took another step.

Pippa. Green eyes, smiling. Forgiving. I looked down at him again, this time a little closer. His hair hung across his cheek and stuck fast with sweat. I could tell he had tried to cut it once, probably with a sharp shell, by the ragged line above his eyes. He didn't have a partner who could make braids like mine could. There were ugly bruises on his outstretched legs, the sign of a thief who had attempted to steal on more than one occasion.

His opposite arm was pinned to the ground by an arrow. By the churned sand around him I guessed he had struggled all afternoon to pull himself out. Under the soft sand countless roots reached deep to anchor the grasses against the ocean. Now they were holding the arrow as well.

Thief's good hand changed from *Mercy* to an open palm. *Friendship.* Despite myself I returned the sign. I stepped into his furrow, groaning at the pain in my leg. When I gripped the end of the shaft sticking up from his arm he screamed in agony and thrashed at me with his legs.

"Don't move, you idiot!" I shouted. "If I fall down, I'm not getting back up and you know what that means." He caught my meaning, if not my words, and his thrashing stopped.

He whimpered.

There was only one way to get him free. One of the ends of the arrow would have to be broken in order to pull it through the flesh. I leaned over him and scooped away as much sand as I could, so that more of the stick was exposed. I began to bend it. Tears streamed down his face as he leaned with me. There was a crackling sound and the end suddenly broke cleanly between my hands.

I pointed at his good arm. "Help me pull." I motioned to him again and he brought his good hand over to grip the feathered end. His face went as white as the sea birds calling above us, but he held on with determination. Putting my good foot against his arm and clenching the stick below the feathers, we began to pull the arrow free.

"More!"

He fainted as the shaft pulled loose of his arm and I lost my balance, swinging my arms wildly about as I hopped crazily to keep from falling. Bran's chicken popped into my head and in the strangeness of the moment I gave a painful gasp of a laugh. When I had my balance back I sent the arrow spinning off into the furrows.

He retched and sat up. Then, white-faced and soaking with sweat, Thief stood, holding his arm tight against his chest. When he noticed the oncoming sea, he started babbling in gasps.

"I know, I know," I said. I pointed to the caves, now only vague dark blotches in the dim light. He nodded, slipping his good arm under my shoulder. He smelled bad, as if he had relieved himself. If it weren't for the wind gusting around us, I would have had a difficult time handling the pain and the horrible smell.

Thief was almost my height, and strong. Between

us we cut the distance to the caves in half, stopping only briefly to rest. I noticed that he had not changed his habits, for each time we rested he would bend down and search a body.

A Spear lay on his back with an arrow sticking out from his neck, just below the tip of his mask. Thief scrambled over to him. "Come on, Thief." I tugged him forward. It frightened me to see even a dead Spear, but Thief continued to paw at the dark robes for a moment before standing, grinning, with a bunch of shiny keys that jingled and flashed. I pulled on his arm again. We had to reach the caves before all light was gone. There were no torches out for us at the Mouth, and when the sun was gone completely we would have no hope of finding our way in the darkness.

Step . . . *jingle* . . . step . . . *jingle* . . . With every drag of my leg the keys in Thief's hand rattled, until I began counting the jingles instead of steps to keep the pain out of my head. After so many strides that I lost count, the ocean finally caught up to us. As it rushed over our feet we yelled at the same time. The sand, so firmly packed after a day of settling in the hot sun, softened instantly in the water. Our feet sank in the mire. Thief dropped his arm lower to my waist and we plunged on.

At the foot of the mountain the sand gave way to stone and we changed our careful stepping into a painful lope, desperately trying to make our way to higher ground. When at last we reached the final path leading up to the Mouth, the tide was swirling at my knees.

The waves struck with more force now, and with the sun all but gone I became terrified we were not going to make the last twenty strides. The path was wide enough to allow three people to stand side by side, but as the water surged ten strides ahead of us, we had to guess each step. Just an arm's length away from safety, my good leg missed the path. We fell sideways into the water. I had to kick with only one leg, and ended up twisting onto my back and floating, rather than struggle with direction. The first waves sucked me away from the Mouth. Too exhausted to fight, I let the next surge rush me toward the cliffs. The light was dim when I cranked my head around. All I could see was the nearest wall of the mountain. I threw one arm behind me to protect my head.

The surge threw me up against smooth rock. I grabbed

desperately at the slippery stone, trying to hold on to anything that would keep me from being dragged out again. I missed. But as my body slid uselessly down toward the sea, a hand suddenly seized my hair. I was yanked higher. I kicked with my leg and grasped at the rock. With each finger of height I gained, the waves crashed and the hand pulled harder on my hair. With a final burst of strength I scrambled above the water and an arm looped under my shoulder to hoist me up onto dry ground.

In the near darkness all I could see were shining teeth. Thief laughed and yammered away excitedly, rubbing my hair from time to time while I lay back, my chest heaving for air. The sea salt stung my wound horribly. If the cold hadn't numbed me, I likely would have fainted again. I breathed gratefully, staring up at the night sky while the waves just below thundered angrily.

Now that we had reached the Mouth I would have to walk again—but could I? I put my hands down to the arrow and gently felt around the area, trying hard not to think about blood or broken bones. From what I could tell, the sharp end had struck me from behind, toward the side of my thigh, and passed through to the front. It was a bad wound, but at least it had gone through the side of my leg and not the middle. I needed to get to Pippa and Tia. They would figure out what to do.

Thief never stopped talking the entire time. It was likely very good advice he was giving me, but I couldn't understand a word, and since pain was the only thing on my mind I just wanted silence. In only a few days I had made more friends than I had ever known in my life, and already I wanted one of them to shut up.

"Shut up," I groaned.

"Shut up?"

"Yes, shut up."

"Shut up, shut up, shut up!" he sang. Either he was delirious or too numb to feel any pain in his arm.

"Thief," I cut him off, "we have to go to Pippa and the others. They will help us."

"Thief?"

"Thief, Thief, Thief. *You* are a thief. Now shut up and let's go to Pippa."

He nudged my arm. "Shut Up," he repeated. Then he thumped his own chest. "Thief."

I groaned and leaned forward. Although I didn't want

to get near the water again I knew that the cold would numb the pain and allow me to walk. When I tried dipping my leg into the water, Thief latched onto my arm so I wouldn't fall. After several minutes of holding my leg in cold water, I pulled it out and held on to his good arm while he bathed his own injury. He yelped when it touched the water and for once fell silent.

On our feet again, we hobbled along the cliff face in the direction of the Mouth. Within a few moments we found the final edge of the path leading to the large cave itself. Ocean spray blasted up from time to time, falling like a light rain as we walked. Above us the sea birds called their evening song and flew like blurry ghosts in the night sky.

At the entrance we both froze. All my life I had walked through the Mouth in daylight, almost always escorted by Spears and with Pippa by my side. Now at night, with a thief, and darkness all around, I hesitated at stepping into the blackness. The wind whipped at our backs and the crashing ocean echoed wildly down the tunnel, making it impossible to hear any voices on the inside. I pictured Pippa lying afraid in our cell. Was she safe? Were Bran and Tia with her?

"Let's go, Thief." I gripped his shoulder tighter.

"Shut Up, Thief, go," he said and stepped forward.

"My name is Coriko," I groaned. "It is *Cor-i-ko.* Not Shut Up. Understand?"

"*Cor-ee-ko,*" he repeated.

I have walked across those cold stones thousands of times before, so even in the pitch darkness my unsteady feet knew where to go. At the end of the long Neck tunnel, the caves branch to the upper and lower levels, the dividing line between the Onesies' and the Twosies' cells. Without speaking we moved at the only pace we had left in us, shuffling up the walkway, feeling along the walls until we reached the cell chambers.

It was foolish, I suppose, for us to walk into our own prisons, but I guessed that Thief was as anxious as I was to reach his cell and hear a familiar voice. I didn't know if he had a plan. Pippa would have. I certainly didn't—I just wanted to be home.

The noise of the ocean lessened once the path rose and took us into the cells. Warmth, sweat, dry grass—smells from all of the things that had been my home wafted around me in a split second and a lump grew in my throat.

But unlike the usual murmuring from hundreds of voices, there was absolute silence.

"Pippa!" I whispered frantically into the blackness. No answer.

"Feelah!" Thief called beside me.

We stood uncertain, leaning against each other and waiting. This was supposed to be the end of our miserable journey from the fields to the caves. I had expected Pippa to answer and call me over, stroking my hair and soothing my pain. No Pippa. No Feelah.

Thief whimpered. We stood for what felt like an entire sleep, until my leg suddenly began to spasm. It gave out and sent me crashing to the hard stone floor.

When I came to my senses again, blood was pounding in my head and Thief was whispering harshly, trying to silence me. "Shaw, shaw, shaw, Coreeko. Shaw, shaw, shaw."

I shut my mouth tight as I felt another scream rising into my throat. Putting my hand down to my injured leg, I felt for the arrow. It was gone. I sat up slowly, allowing the swirling to stop before I made a more thorough check of my leg. The work-cloth was now tightly bound right around my leg, so tight that I couldn't slip my fingers underneath. And the arrow was truly gone from both ends.

"How did you do that, Thief?"

He chuckled, rumbling something in his singsong language. The tightness of the cloth helped ease the pain, and although the throbbing continued, I didn't feel so dizzy-weak anymore. I lay back, closing my eyes and smelling the damp grasses in the cells. There was moisture near my head, a trickle of water beside my cheek. I lapped at it greedily and encouraged Thief to do the same, even though he couldn't understand me.

Then I must have dozed, for when Thief called to me again I stirred awake.

"Coreeko . . . Coreeko." I felt his arms under my shoulders, urging me with a persistence he had never shown before. "Thief, Coreeko . . . go." A light from somewhere behind, somewhere back in the Neck, caught my attention immediately. But what startled me far more than the growing brightness was the sound of voices—men's voices. I gripped Thief's arm tighter. "Those are *men*!" I hissed.

In the dim light I could just make out his hand signal: *Spears?*

"Maybe." I shook my head. Then I passed my hand over my head to signal *Outside.*

He stared back, eyes wide. We had to find Pippa and the others. If the Outside had come and entered the caves . . .

I started hobbling toward the light, but Thief took hold of my arm before I had gone three steps and turned me around slowly. He was pointing in the opposite direction, farther into the cells, and jabbering excitedly. "Feelah . . . Pippa!"

Every morning when we left our cells the Spears turned us down into the Neck. We never went the other way. And now for the first time I followed Thief's pointing finger to the opposite direction, into darkness. I had always assumed it was just a dead end, but now as we stood on a part of the path farther down from our cell than I had ever been, I saw that the glistening stone formed another tunnel.

A second outburst of shouting from behind set our legs moving in the direction of the new tunnel, shuffling and slipping on the wet stone. We had already crawled into our own prison—there was no sense in giving ourselves up again. But the new route ended almost as quickly as we turned the corner. I found my nose pressed up against a hard, slimy door. Its rough surface made me think of the driftwood Pippa and I sometimes threw into the sea at the beach.

Thief was doing his own exploring. When he gave a gasp I looked where his hands had come to rest. A long piece of wood—much thicker than a prod, at the height of our chests—was set across the main part of the door. It was held in place by cold, metal hooks that curved upward like cupped hands.

Thief wrestled a moment with the bar before it slid out from the metal and fell to the floor with a thump. We stood frozen for a moment, listening, then both grabbed at the door. It swung toward us with a groan. We eased it to the wall as quietly as we could, then turned to face the opening.

A cold, salty wind blew against our faces from some darkness ahead.

Thief slapped my back encouragingly. "Coreeko, go."

I nodded and stepped forward, careful to feel for any

dips in the floor. My mind was racing as fast as my heart. What did the Spears keep in this tunnel? Did it lead down to the sea, or farther back into the mountain? Were there Spears inside waiting for us to stumble into them? Despite my fear there was another, more powerful, question that made me press ahead, step by painful step: Where was Pippa?

Several times we passed openings of coldness on our left. I realized that these must be tunnels to the ocean roaring loudly from below. I stuck closely to the wall on my right. We appeared to be moving slowly upward, with the tunnel making a gentle curve away from the caves.

The walls were damp and slimy as we felt our way into the darkness. Several times I lost my balance on the slippery floor. And yet, as we walked, the sound of the ocean gradually became fainter and the stones at my fingertips felt less slimy. After many, many steps the cold air was gradually replaced by a warm wind. I stood straight to let it bathe my face.

Thief bumped into me from behind. "Coreeko?"

"All is well, Thief. Can you feel it? There are two tunnels now."

He breathed in as the air hit him.

"Which way?" I asked.

"Coreeko, go." He touched my left shoulder. I wanted to go immediately, to let the warm wind comfort us, but something deep inside told me that Pippa was at the end of the tunnel on the right. I hesitated. The warm air was coming down to us, which meant that in the left tunnel we would be climbing even farther away from the caves. If Pippa, Bran, and Tia had not been in the Twosies' cells, then they must have been moved to the lower chambers. There was no time for exploring. I was about to step to the right when Thief found my face with his hands and purposely placed two fingers on both my eyes.

"Thief, Coreeko . . ." He pressed on my eyes again.

Hmmm. *Take a look.* He wanted us to see what was out there. It was a powerful temptation to follow the warm air to its source, to catch one glimpse—to see Outside.

"Fine, we will look. Then we hurry back."

The breeze grew stronger as we hobbled up the steep path. I opened my mouth to let in as much air as I could. It warmed me to my toes. Even my soaking work-cloth was drying quickly in the breeze. It flapped gently with each step forward. From somewhere ahead a dim light was shining across the rocky floor, and for the first time in what seemed like ages I could see my hands in front of me again.

A sudden gust brought sand spinning into the tunnel. I closed my eyes as it beat against my forehead. The desert! I quickened my pace, feeling a little guilty that we were probably moving farther from Pippa, but unable to resist a peek at what had only been a dream all my life. The light increased as we turned a bend, and in a heartbeat we stumbled on the opening without any warning other than the warmer air around us.

Thief came and stood beside me, swaying giddily at the height and looking down onto Outside. A bright moon shone, lighting up the sea to our left and displaying a darkness that I first took to be giant round stones stretching outward from the arm of the mountains. The shape reminded me of something . . . A clean, earthy kind of smell I had never known before wafted up from below. I breathed deeply. "Trees," I said out loud. "Pippa's trees." There was a path, narrow and steep, beside the cave. It looked as if it led down the mountain and away from the desert, toward the sea. For a brief moment I felt a wild rush to scream, to yell the word "freedom" out to the desert, to rush down the trail to a new world.

Thief growled and I turned to my right. His face was lit by a light far brighter than the moon, and when I gazed below to find its source I stifled a cry. The entire land was on fire. Torches flared into the night like the brilliant yellow heads of the grasses at midday.

There were fires on the mountain as well. Only fifty strides away from us, and slightly below, flames flickered off the masked faces of Spears who stood still as stone, looking down over Outside. Their dark capes fluttered in the breeze. Their spears and helmets glinted in the moonlight like firelight on a wet wall. Most of them were standing with their weapons pointing out to the enemy far below, but dotted here and there among the stones I could see resting forms with their backs against the mountainside. Behind a cluster of them I could see a larger darkness. Another tunnel. I shook my head. The mountain must be riddled with them.

The Spears were definitely outnumbered. For every Spear I could see, there were a hundred more torches burning fiercely below. But they still had an advantage. From the heights the Spears could throw things down onto their attackers and hide behind boulders on the rocky slopes. There were no trees and not many stones to hide behind at the foot of the southern slope, only flat desert that disappeared into darkness at the horizon.

The Outsiders were thickest directly below and to the right, where the desert met the Hollow and the tunnels that led into the cliffs. Although I had only stood before them once in my life, the enormous bars, as thick as my arms, had haunted my dreams from the time I first arrived. From the base of the gates the Outsiders gradually fanned out to fill the whole plain like the sand in the desert. It was no wonder that the death clouds had seemed to fill the sky.

I wondered why the Outsiders hadn't bothered to come up our way, or to enter the Hollow and find the smaller caves to enter into the heart of Grassland. Or had they, and that was where the clouds of arrows had come from before? My eyes quickly began searching the rocks around us. Peering directly downward from our hiding spot I suddenly saw why we were all alone. The mountain turned into sheer cliffs below our feet, so steep that only a bird could find its way up. But it certainly didn't stop arrows. All around I began to see the wicked sticks in the moonlight, lying broken on the ground, or sticking out of crevices in the rock. I glanced up fearfully.

I turned sharply around as something moved only a stone's throw to our right. It was a Spear, shuffling and poking at a cluster of dark forms. I gasped as the twisted shapes of men—some Spears, some from Outside—lying cold and silent in death, flashed into view with each movement of the Spear's torch. He was gathering weapons from the fallen, rolling each one over with his foot before moving on to the next.

I realized that one battle had already been fought. The Spears must have used the tunnel to beat the Outsiders back down any slopes they had been able to climb.

I glanced at Thief. Even in the dim light I could see that his dark face had taken on a shade of gray. It was a good thing I couldn't see my own. The Spear made a sudden motion and I jerked my head back. He raised an arm, waved it several times, and shouted, pointing down onto the plain. After my initial shock of hearing a Spear voice I stiffened as all the lights on the mountainside winked out together within a heartbeat of each other.

I crouched instinctively and felt Thief do the same. In the darkness and silence that followed, he moved even closer to me, so that I could actually hear his breathing as he sucked in and held.

A harsh voice, commanding and fierce, suddenly called out from the plain far below. It echoed up into the hills toward us. The tone was so terrifying that I felt as if it was trying to reach me. The torches nearest the voice moved all at once in a blur of motion and a noise like a rushing wind blotted out the voice as it cried again. A moment later a whistling sound made us look up. In the face of the moon we saw sticks by the hundreds go hurtling up into the night.

7

I RIPPED AT THIEF'S ARM, TURNED, and hopped wildly back to the shelter of the tunnel, holding one hand above my head and praying every prayer I could ever remember Pippa saying. Thief pounded in after me just as the first arrows landed behind us, skidding and slashing against the mountainside.

Heedless of the noise we were making, we scrambled into the darkness and security of our cave, desperate to put as much distance between us and the arrows as we could. At the place where the two tunnels forked I turned down the one we hadn't come up, the one we thought might lead downward to the lower cages. I slowed my pace only slightly as I fought to keep my fear and the pain in my leg from taking control. Soon the floor became slippery once again, and my hands were quickly covered in slime as I felt my way along the wall in the darkness.

"Coreeko!"

When I heard Thief's call, I came to a halt, leaning heavily against the wet rock of the passage. It was good to hear his familiar voice again. He slumped to the floor beside me, his breath coming in heaves.

"I didn't think I could go that fast," I panted, not caring that he couldn't understand me. "Sorry."

He grunted.

When my heart finally began to slow I reached out for his hand at my feet.

He pulled back in pain. "Yahhh, Coreeko!"

"Sorry. Wrong arm." I reached out again, more carefully this time. I pointed his hand in the direction we were facing. "Feelah? Pippa?"

He grunted again. "Feelah, Pippa."

If Thief was right, the Spears used these tunnels to get from the upper and lower caves without having to use the Neck or the Mouth. Gritting my teeth at the pain, I pushed away from the wall and stumbled farther into the cool passage.

Walking downhill with my stiff leg turned my steps into jerky hops that sent waves of pain through my body. Eventually I had to walk with my injured leg going forward first, one painful step at a time. Thief followed close behind, muttering and whispering at me as if his words would help make the slope less slippery. Several times I had to stop and rest, pressing my face against the cool rock to stop the raging in my head. A fever was beginning to work its way through me and I felt the strength drain from every limb.

At one point Thief stepped past me and took the lead. Gripping my hand in his own, he led me gently until the slope evened out and I was able to walk more easily on my own. And then, abruptly, he stopped.

"Ahhh, Coreeko," he crooned softly. "Feelah, Pippa."

I put my hand up in front of me and felt another wooden door, almost exactly like the one that had released us from the Twosies' cells. A shiver of anticipation ran through me, and despite the pain and the fever a smile broke out on my face. "Well done, Thief."

"Heh, heh, Coreeko." He laughed softly.

We both felt for the crosspiece of wood. Together we lifted it off the hooks and eased it to the floor.

I could smell them the moment we stepped into the cave—the heat from hundreds of bodies, all crammed into the lower cages, blew against us. The murmur of many voices whispered fearfully to one another in the blackness. As we crept forward I listened with each step for any sound other than a Digger. At one spot in the center of the main passage we both stopped, hardly breathing, terribly aware that we were the only ones not behind the bars. Somewhere among them—I dared to hope—Pippa was sleeping in the protection of Bran and Tia.

"Coreeko," Thief suddenly whispered directly in my ear, gripping my shoulders at the same time.

"What?"

"Thief, Feelah. Coreeko, Pippa." I felt his arm fall away from my shoulder and I nodded in the dark. It was time for us to find our mates. He found my hand and pressed his palm firmly against mine, mumbling some soft words.

"Thank you, Thief," I whispered back. "I will find you soon."

"Go, Coreeko." He was gone.

I limped up to the nearest cage and called softly for

Pippa. There was movement, then someone leaned up against the bars.

"Heh?" A Onesie, by the sound of him.

I moved on to the next cage, and to the next after that. Behind me the people I had awakened were coming to the realization that a Digger was outside of the cages. They began whispering and calling to me, urging me with words I didn't understand. By the time I had passed twenty cages the noise behind me was deafening, and my sense of desperation grew with every stride. Thief had obviously caused the same disturbance on the other end, for shouts broke out ahead of me. If the Spears heard the racket and headed for us . . . I *had* to find Pippa!

"Pippa!" I yelled. It didn't matter now. The Spears, if there were any in the caves at all, wouldn't have known who was yelling and who was not. I could only hope they were too far away to return.

"Coriko!" More beautiful than the cool waters on a hot day, Bran's voice echoed from several cages away. I lurched forward, calling into the cages as I passed, moving faster than I had thought possible on a ruined leg.

Then warm hands were grabbing at me, touching my

hair, and Pippa's wet face was pushing through the bars, kissing me wherever she could find a free spot. I put my hand through, crushing her head to my chest, and with my other hand grasped Tia's and Bran's hands. I could only lean against the bars, not ever getting enough of their comfort.

"Coriko. How . . . Where did you come from?" Tia finally managed.

I was crying so hard I couldn't speak.

Pippa wrestled herself from my embrace and managed to grip my face in her hands. "Shhh. All's well now, Corki. Peace."

We pressed our foreheads together and I blocked out the shouts and noise of all the others, aware only of Pippa and her calming voice.

"How is your leg?"

So many thoughts were pouring through me at once that what came out of my mouth was a garbled retelling. "Thief helped me . . . Pulled out the arrow . . . I was going to *drown* him, Pippa, but he helped me . . . Torches on the desert . . ." My last words came out as a whisper. "I have seen Outside."

"Corki, is your leg all right?" She felt for the cloth

around my thigh. I heard her suck in a breath when she couldn't find the arrow. She reached back up and stroked my head. "Corki. Peace. Try to be calm. Think quietly."

I was ready to collapse, but I tried to do as she asked, to breathe deeply. "There is a tunnel . . . back there, that leads to our cells . . . and to Outside. There is an army in the desert, at the Hollow. There are many more Outsiders than Spears. I saw dead Spears everywhere."

Bran broke in. "Are the Outside people in the caves?"

"No." I shook my head. "I don't think so. We didn't see any. The Spears won't let them in. But the things you called arrows keep coming and I don't know if it will be long before Outside does get in. There are so many of them." I shivered.

"What else did you see?" Pippa whispered.

"Trees, Pippa! I saw your trees. Near the ocean . . . away from the fighting."

"Were they nice?"

"Yes, I think so. It was dark. But they smelled so good."

"Now what are we going to do?" Bran stomped impatiently. "He's out there, and we're in here."

Tia slid closer. "We need to get out, Coriko. We think—" She hesitated. "We think they might send a First Cleansing if the Spears don't win. Pippa guesses that if the soldiers from Outside get through the Mouth, the Spears will try to drown them . . . and us, too. She thinks that—"

"We must hurry, Corki," Pippa finished. The noise of hundreds of frightened Diggers broke back into my calm. I leaned my head heavily against the bars and tried to think. I hadn't thought of what to do once I got here. All I wanted was to reach Pippa, and then sleep, sleep peacefully for a long time in the company of my friends, where my leg could heal and I wouldn't have to fear . . . just for a while.

"Is there anything out there that we could use to open the bars, Coriko?" Tia was trying hard to keep her voice from breaking. "Coriko?"

"Coriko!" Bran's voice shook me awake.

There was something I needed to remember. "But can't I just . . . ?"

Pippa stroked my hair. "When we are safe . . . When we get to the trees, you will sleep for a long time and I will bring you good food. But we need you to do a little more, Corki. Just a little more."

Her soothing voice worked into my fuzzy mind. I wiped at my face, sat up straighter, and nodded. "I'll look around. But I don't know how we can open the bars. The Spears all have—" I stopped in midsentence. "Thief!" I screamed at the top of my voice. "Thief!"

I broke away from Pippa's hands and hopped along the length of the cages, calling as I went. Diggers grabbed at me and I had to take several steps away or someone would have pinned me to the bars. The noise was thunderous, and I was trying to yell above them all when I bashed into someone directly in front of me.

"Coreeko," he grunted. It was Thief.

"Thief! Thief, the keys! Do you still have the keys?"

"Coreeko . . . Feelah!" he yelled. The next thing I knew he had gripped my hand and was putting it on his face. But it wasn't his face. As my fingers moved around I felt a wide nose, much wider than the Thief's. A girl giggled and I felt the mouth turn into a smile.

"Feelah? But how—?"

There was a jingling beside my ear. "Heh, heh, Coreeko."

I hugged them both so hard I heard them gasp above

the roar of the Diggers. We held hands all the way back to the others.

"Pippa! Stand back from the bars," I shouted.

Bran was frantic. "Coriko. What do you have? Did you find something?"

"I found the best thing!"

Thief stepped past me, and after an eternal moment the door creaked open. My friends crowded around while the others in the cage stumbled out blindly into the dark. Bran threw his arms around my waist and tried to lift me off the ground.

"Put me down, Bran," I gasped. I introduced Thief and Feelah as best as I could. Then I felt Tia's hand on my head.

"Enough! Coriko, we must go now. We have no idea how much time we have to get out of here."

"She's right." Pippa had found my hand. "We must go." She tugged at me. "As soon as we release the others."

Bran stopped pumping Thief on the back. "The others? No, Pippa. That will bring the Spears for sure."

"Let's go," Tia urged, pushing us ahead a few steps

with her long arms. Thief gripped my arm. Pippa held my hand tighter.

I opened my mouth to speak, but the voices around us grew strangely quiet. A flicker of wind struck my face and with it came a horrifying realization. "The Cleansing."

Tia broke from our terror first, pushing us to the right in the direction of the new door, and screaming for us to run. Pippa jerked away from my hand without a warning. Thief's keys jangled above the din and I knew in a heartbeat that she had them. As I tried to fight against the others to find her again I heard her call out, "We've got to shut the door or they're going to drown." The jangling of the keys faded away from me.

Someone's arm ended up in my mouth and my own fingers poked into a face as we jostled each other for a direction. With a final burst I broke away, screaming out Pippa's name and trying to hobble in the general direction of the Mouth.

"Coriko," Bran yelled. "What are you doing?"

"Follow Thief! He'll show you where to go!" I don't know if he heard me but I couldn't risk even a heartbeat to find out. I hadn't moved twenty strides when the heavy wind hit, throwing me off balance on my shaky leg. I knew I was stumbling to my death. Pippa had made the final decision for us by running toward the Cleansing, but all I could think of was reaching her before the water struck. Keeping the wind in my face I threw my leg forward one painful leap at a time, desperately hoping I wouldn't miss her in the darkness.

"Pippa!"

"Here!"

I tripped on her two strides later and found her struggling wildly with something against the wall.

"It's the door, Corki! We've got to shut the door!"

I reached out blindly and found the edge of the soaking wood. Squeezing in between the wall and the door I pushed with all my might, desperate to get it closed before the water struck. But the heavy timbers didn't move so much as a shard. "I can't . . . I can't . . . ," I grunted.

Pippa sobbed with effort beside me.

"Coriko!" It was Bran. He shoved his shoulder up next to mine.

"Push!" I yelled. With all of us pushing, I felt the difference immediately. The mighty door moved, swinging on its rusty hinges into the wind. We pushed it as far as it would go before I remembered that we needed the crosspiece to hold it in place. Without it we would be swept away once the tidewater reached us.

"Hold on." I dropped to the floor and groped frantically over the slimy stone, but there was nothing to be found except clumps of seaweed and broken sticks. "Where would they keep it?" I screeched in frustration. I began to feel the wall, hoping desperately that they might have attached it there, when my fingers touched wood. It was the beam!

"It's too high up," I yelled. "I can't get it down. It's being held by something."

"Let me try!" a new voice called from behind. Tia! Her hands touched mine as she tried to gain a hold on the crosspiece. The wood lifted for a second, then fell back down.

"Hurry!" Bran gasped. "I can hear the water."

With a final heave she lifted the beam from the wall. It clattered to the stone floor. We found it quickly, hoisted it up and slammed it into place behind the metal hooks.

"Get back," Tia commanded.

I could hear the other two scramble away and in a moment the thunder of the water became louder than the cries of the Diggers behind us. At the last moment I threw my hands up to protect my face as the roaring ocean struck the door.

"It's holding!" Bran yelled above the noise.

The wood creaked and groaned under the pressure, and a small stream spilled over our feet from a crack at the bottom.

"We are leaving. Now!" Tia called us quickly to her. "Pippa, you may unlock the cages as we go. Do not wait to see if the Diggers open them. Bran, help her. I will take Coriko as fast as he can go. Move *now*!"

There was no questioning her authority. She slipped her arm under my shoulders and I leaned on her gratefully, limping for the opposite end of the caves toward the new tunnel. The Diggers needed no explanation when the cages began to open. They poured out from behind the bars like a school of frightened fish, following our voices toward the last remaining door.

"Pippa! Bran!" Tia yelled over our shoulders.

"How long will it hold, Tia?"

She shifted her arm on my shoulder. Diggers began knocking into us in their haste to get by. “It better last for a while longer. If the other Diggers keep passing us, by the time we get to your new tunnel there is going to be a mess of people in the way.” She tried to help me by brushing bodies aside when they came too close.

And where *was* safety? The last time Thief and I had stumbled out the end of the new tunnel, we had almost been killed by arrows.

“Tia! Where are you?” I could hear Bran screaming somewhere directly behind us.

“Bran!” We both yelled. We waited, calling out back and forth, until Pippa and Bran found their way to us.

“I got every cage,” Pippa gasped.

Without hesitating Tia picked up the pace and started an awkward lope forward into the darkness. Her arm gripped me tighter. “You’ve got to go faster, Coriko!”

I tried not to limp and turned my jog into an agonized run. There was no one around us anymore, although I could hear shouts up ahead. Then a sudden crash came from behind and the roar of the ocean filled our ears.

“Oh no, oh no!” Bran groaned.

My side suddenly scraped against the wall of the new tunnel, and a hand gripped the neck of my work-cloth.

"Coreeko!" Thief helped me through the door.

Tia sprawled forward, knocking me out of Thief's helpful grip and landing on top of me. My head began swirling and Tia's weight on my leg sent me into a darkness deeper than the blackness around us.

8

I WOKE UP WITH MY HEAD ON someone's lap.

"Hello, Coriko," Bran whispered.

"Pippa—" I croaked.

"She's helping Tia try to talk with Thief and Feelah. She left only a moment ago, I just took over because you hadn't woken up yet."

"What happened?"

He sighed. "Thief managed to shut the door after we came through. He and Feelah put the crosspiece in place and stopped the water. Pippa fixed up your leg again and then we just sat around and waited. Nobody knows what to do."

"Hmph," I grunted and sat up slowly. My bandage

had been retied and it felt a little better to have it so tight again. "We must go to the trees."

"That is what Pippa said."

Tia and Pippa returned shortly. To our surprise they didn't just bring Thief and Feelah. There were whispers and whimpers from a large crowd in the darkness behind us.

"They don't know where to go," Pippa explained as she hugged me. "They just follow whoever makes a move." In the blackness of the tunnel it was impossible to tell how many there were, but from the sounds of them I guessed that it was a large number.

"Trees," Pippa was saying excitedly. "I can smell them already."

"But what about the soldiers from Outside?" Bran piped up. "And Spears? What about all of them?"

"Thief and I didn't get spotted the last time," I whispered. "Maybe we can do it again. The path we saw to the trees leads away from the battle anyway, down toward the ocean."

"We must go with caution," Tia said. "Thief," she hissed. "Come up here to the front with me."

Following the same tunnel that had led us to the others, we made our way back up the narrow passage. At the fork we kept to the side that headed upward toward the desert. As we approached the tunnel opening, the first glimmer of moonlight shone on the walls ahead. A sudden thought struck me. I turned to stare back at the frightened faces.

"Where are all the other Threesies and Foursies that were in your group?" I asked Tia.

"They were taken away the first night, before the Spears put us in the cages," she whispered back.

"Why now? Outside is attacking."

"I think . . . I think the Spears were going to use them to help fight. It may be why they were brought here in the first place."

Thief signed *Silence* and I risked a quick whisper to the others. "We are very close to the opening that looks onto the desert. Remember, there may be Spears near the entrance."

Our ragged group moved like crabs across the sand as we crept toward the opening.

"How do you say *Stop*?" Tia suddenly whispered in my ear. I gave her a puzzled stare and then showed her the hand signal. "Only a few of us should go look," she said. "The rest should wait in the tunnel."

She raised her hands into the glint of light against the wall and the group froze. She then pointed to Thief, to herself, and finally toward the tunnel opening. Thief nodded and started immediately, keeping close to the right-hand side of the cave wall. Tia gave us each a quick smile, then turned and left silently after him. Pippa wrapped her arms around me and we crouched down to wait.

"What if there are soldiers waiting for us to come out?" she whispered.

I clenched my teeth and strained my eyes ahead to see any sign of movement. "Pray that there aren't."

For what seemed like hours we waited. The light grew stronger in the cave from the early morning sun breaking the horizon. I looked back at the dirty, strained faces peering anxiously up at us, and sighed.

"How are we going to get down to the trees with all of them?" I whispered to Pippa. "We'll be spotted in a heartbeat."

"I've been thinking about that." She leaned her cheek against my arm. "We've heard no shouts, no soldiers or

Spears yelling orders. My heart tells me that the battle is over. When we go out into the blue sky, I think we will find many things we were not expecting."

I waited for her to say more, but nothing came. With nothing to do for the moment I became aware again of my leg and the ugly throbbing that pounded in my head. A little moan escaped before I could stop it. Pippa sat up to rub my back.

"Hurry up, hurry *up*," Bran muttered. Behind us the other Diggers stirred restlessly. When two of them, probably cellmates, approached us, Bran and I frowned. Pippa smiled at them and signed an open palm.

Go now? The larger one kept his focus on Pippa.

She shook her head. *Peace. Stay. Spears and danger. Go wait.* Satisfied, the two sat back down.

My head was just beginning to droop when a scrabbling sound caused me to jerk awake. Two dark figures, their faces hidden by shadow, crept toward us from the lip of the opening. I reached behind me for a rock, or anything I could use to throw.

"This way," Tia's voice hissed at us. "Silently."

Bran was on his feet before she had even finished. His

movement caused a ripple of excitement to spread down the tunnel.

"Silently!" she commanded again and raised her hands. Despite my pain I felt a little smile twitch as I watched her turn back toward the entrance. It *was* good to have a Threesie with us.

My leg had stiffened in the long wait, and I needed Pippa's support to start walking. The last twenty paces to the top of the tunnel entrance felt almost as bad as when the arrow had first hit me, and Bran was forced to put an arm under my shoulder as well. I could feel him trembling—from fear or excitement, I couldn't tell—and found myself staring ahead for dark-cloaked figures.

"Crouch down," Tia hissed as we passed from the shadows of the cave to the open sky. The morning light wrapped itself around us and the warm desert wind sent our work-cloths flapping. I lifted my arms from Bran and Pippa and leaned forward on the cliff edge to look down the mountain. The desert floor was crawling with long lines of men streaming in and out of Grassland, like ants about a hill. As my eyes adjusted to the light I saw wagons burdened to overflowing making their way back across the sands from where they had come.

"That looks like it could be shards." Pippa squinted down at the wagons, her voice sounding hollow. "They are carrying our shards away."

The wagons formed a long line, heading straight across the desert floor. In the light I could now see a narrow track, not much wider than the cave paths, leading as far as the horizon. But unlike our paths, it did not look well traveled. Somehow the Outsiders must have followed the Spears back.

The Outsiders had come prepared. Each wagon had two large animals at the front of it—horses I guessed, if Pippa's descriptions were correct—with high sides in order to heap more goods into the back. We could hear the creak of their giant wheels and the shouting of the drivers even from way up where we were. There were colored tents of many sizes spread out everywhere I looked. Soldiers were passing in and out of them, carrying burdens and packing up their weapons of war.

I felt a nudge from Bran and turned my attention to the mountainside itself. I followed his pointing finger to the hundreds of dark bodies lying lifeless among the rocks. The Spears had not lasted long. A group of four or five lay sprawled where they had fallen, with the shafts of arrows still sticking up from their backs. Two of them were missing helmets. I sucked in a breath when I looked at their faces. They looked like Foursies.

Tia crept up close enough to whisper, "Stay low. The soldiers will see movement even from this distance away. There is a road." She pointed back over her shoulder. "And a smaller trail. It is quite close. Probably too close. We must keep the younger ones silent."

"Won't they see us on the trail?" Bran asked.

"Not if we stay very low. There's pretty good cover. But let's go. You'll see in a moment anyway."

"Coreeko, Pippa." Thief waved us on, and I tore my eyes away from the wagons. He was kneeling off to the side of the tunnel entrance, beckoning us to follow him. Many of the Diggers were already streaming past him, not caring to look at the disaster and wanting only to find a safer place to hide along the trail.

The path that Thief and I had found earlier was not the only way down, as the growing daylight now showed us. The trail Tia had seen, cleverly hidden and well groomed, had been cut twenty strides beside the wider trail she called a road. It must have maddened Outside to discover the trail after the battle was over. Unless, of course, it was the way they finally got in. A few soldiers continued to march from the beach back up to the desert, trudging wearily in twos or threes. But our trail followed a natural enormous crack in the side of the mountain, with huge stone walls that provided excellent cover as long as we stayed crouched low. That was probably what kept it so hidden from the desert side—the walls of rock almost making a flap that covered the crevice.

"Why are we going down to the beach when there are many soldiers still coming up from there?" I whispered to Pippa. "This is madness. Let's wait till they are all gone, then go down."

Tia overheard me and leaned her chin up to my ear. "They *are* leaving. You saw the wagons. And I'm pretty sure Thief only saw a few down along the road when he searched. Besides, we can't wait up here. If they search all the tunnels, someone may find us, eventually. At least no soldiers are using the trail right now. As long as we keep quiet we can wait for the last ones to leave and then go hide in the trees. I think we'll be safer there."

To my foggy mind her words made some sense, but I still couldn't help wondering why we were moving toward our enemies instead of away from them. Just before we took our first step onto the narrow trail I mumbled to Pippa, "What do you think?"

She gripped my hand tighter. "I think Tia is right. They would not expect us to go toward them. And I think they should know by now that the caves have been flooded. I imagine they think we are dead. When they finally get inside they will be surprised to find no one there." She gave me a quick smile. "It would not be good to be here when they come looking."

Making our way down the side of the mountain was as painful as it was slow. Pippa was my biggest help. She knew when to stop and let me rest, even when the line of Diggers in front was way ahead, or when the line behind was piling up with frustrated faces. Whenever a soldier or troop marched up the road that ran parallel to us, Tia lifted her hands and we all froze. We crouched up against the hard wall of the mountain, hardly daring to breathe.

Bran whispered encouragement from behind and leaned his hands forward from time to time to steady me.

Even though my heart kept skipping, waiting for that terrible moment of being discovered, I couldn't help noticing the smells. In the furrows, the grasses and the salty sea were the strongest smells I'd ever known. And the desert made me think of cut grasses that had been drying for a long time in the sun. But on the narrow trail, as we moved step by step closer to the distant trees below, the wind was bringing new scents to us—clean, earthy kinds of smells that set my heart hoping, longing, to finally be at the bottom.

After many starts and stops there was an unusually long pause.

"I'm going to see what's happening." Bran's pale face stared back at us. We watched him wade through the tired Diggers and disappear around a bend in the path.

"I am so tired," I whispered.

"Let's sit down," Pippa suggested. The sun had risen higher by now, but was still low in the sky, the walls of our trail casting a cover of shadow over our entire group.

"How are we ever going to get out of here when there

is a whole army out there and we're stuck with this useless lot?" I glanced down the line of ragged Diggers huddled on the trail floor. Like frightened animals their heads kept peering toward the other trail and the looming cliffs above us.

"They deserve the trees as much we do," she said. A while later Bran reappeared, with Tia, Feelah, and Thief following close behind. From the frightened looks on their faces I knew the news was not going to be good.

Tia spoke first. "There is an Outside soldier sleeping on the trail ahead. We've made it down to right where the trail and road get very close together. There's a sort of field there, and I can even see the first trees on the far side. The beach must only be a little ways away. And now somebody with a sword is in our path!" She tried to sound frustrated, but I could tell she was more scared than anything. Thief was looking gray again. I guessed that he had found the man first. Feelah's expression was frozen.

"What now?" Bran asked.

I scowled. "Well, what is he doing?"

"He's just lying there, probably sleeping."

"Maybe he's dead," Pippa suggested.

Tia shook her head. "No. We waited for a while, and he moves."

"So what are we going to do?" Bran repeated.

No one said anything for a moment. I swatted at a bug buzzing near my face and crushed it in my fist. "Kill him," I said. Pippa shot me an angry glance.

"With what?" Tia stared straight back.

Not looking at Pippa I whispered, "With a rock. On the head." There was silence for a moment.

Tia dropped her eyes down to her feet. "I c–can't. I don't want to do it."

I looked at Thief and made the sign for *Outside*, then *Death*. He shook his head vigorously. *No.* Feelah gripped his shoulder.

"No killing," Pippa slapped my arm. "No more." Tia waved at us to be more quiet.

"Well, what are we supposed to do?" I hissed back. "Pat him on the head and wish him happy dreams?" No one said anything so I grumbled, "I'll do it." I took a step forward.

"No killing." Pippa's eyes were pleading now and I couldn't look at them.

"No killing," I muttered, and pulled myself free. "I'll just knock him out."

Tia and Thief stole ahead of us near the end of the line, squeezed past, and patted my head encouragingly. I crept along behind.

The ground finally began to level out, and the smell of wild forest grew stronger than ever. There was green grass only a few strides away, a color I had only seen on seaweed. If I hadn't been so frightened I would have laughed.

Tia suddenly flattened onto her stomach and became completely still. Thief did the same. I crawled forward until I could squeeze in between both of them to take a peek.

Our trail came to an end only ten strides ahead, with the wider trail—a road, by now—finally meeting it on our right. With his hand moving slower than a turtle, Thief lifted a finger and pointed to the tall grass only a stone's throw away. At first I couldn't see anything, but lifting myself up just a little I caught a flash of metal in the morning light. I let out a long slow breath and looked at Tia and Thief. I made the signal for *Danger* and he nodded.

My first thought was to just go back and wait on the trail until the man got up and left with the others. But I couldn't bear the thought of waiting between those closed walls of rock for someone to discover us. There was no place to run on the narrow path. They would finish us off before we could make ten strides. We needed to get to the trees.

I nudged Tia. When she looked at me I motioned to the dirt. I wasn't sure how to get *Rock* through to her, but I was pretty certain she would get the idea. She did. She backed up silently and returned a moment later with a rock that easily filled her whole palm. As she plunked it into my hand I could feel her whole arm trembling. I glanced back at Pippa and regretted it immediately. Tears were streaming down her face and she looked away.

My breath was getting faster and I felt a drip of sweat trickle down my chest. My mouth had gone completely dry and I rubbed the back of my teeth with my tongue nervously. I looked back at the grass, hoping that the man had left while we were waiting for Tia, but the tall stalks stirred restlessly once again and grew still.

I was about to crawl forward when the man coughed.

I fell to the earth as if I'd been struck by an arrow. I scrambled back in between the others and stuffed my hand into my mouth to keep from screaming. When I looked up again, Tia, Bran, Thief, and Pippa were staring beyond me with eyes so wide they could have fallen out and rolled onto the ground. We waited, frozen, as a large dirty hand came above the grasses for a moment and then settled back down.

We had to do something. We had to make a move soon or the soldier might wake up completely. I tested the weight of the rock in my hand for about the tenth time, but no matter how I tried I couldn't get my legs to start moving.

A hand suddenly pressed down firmly on my wrist. Tia reached out and pulled the rock from my fingers, her face dripping with even more sweat than my own. But her lips were pressed firmly together with the same determination I had noticed in her during the First Cleansing. She gripped the rock so tightly that her knuckles turned white.

Watching Tia move toward the soldier was almost as bad as doing it myself. My breathing stopped every time the man made a move, and twice Tia had to freeze and lie flat when soldiers passed by on the road. When she reached the man at last, there was another heart-stopping moment when it looked as if she had fainted. She lay in the grass completely still, with the rock leaning up against her leg. I was about to start after her when she began to move forward again.

Behind us the Diggers had silently joined in, filling the path to overflowing. I held up my hand to signal *Stop* and *Danger*, but they continued to press against us, aware that something was wrong. I turned back to Tia. She was kneeling over the man now, her dark hair standing out against the brightness of the green grass. She held the rock in both hands and slowly raised it above her head.

Beside me, Thief sucked in a breath. I could feel Bran gripping my ankles tight enough to make the pain in my thigh go away. The rock was shaking so violently I worried for a heartbeat that Tia was going to drop it on her own head.

And then the man woke up.

9

BEFORE TIA COULD FINISH HER downward swing the soldier flung up an arm and sent the rock spinning into the grasses. She opened her mouth to scream, but a bloodied hand covered half her face and another caught her arm, pinning it to her side. The soldier was wearing a rounded helmet with a silver noseguard. The rest of his dirty face was covered by a thick stubble of black hair.

Bran jumped over my head before I could even get from my stomach to a crouch. By the time I reached the taller grass, Thief had also passed me. In a moment all I could see were arms and legs rising and falling above the tall stalks. I had been so desperate to help Tia, I had not bothered to look around me as I lunged through their trail of broken grass. But from my standing position it was horrifyingly clear: Everywhere I looked, the field was full of sleeping soldiers with their weapons in hand or lying close beside them. Cloaks, swords, and boots pressed the grasses down like tumbled stones in a field of green. Their bearded faces were hard, deeply lined and frighteningly unforgiving even in their sleep. Although my legs began to move I was certain my heart had long since stopped.

When the man struggling with Tia saw Bran and the Diggers following behind, he opened his mouth to raise the alarm. Just before he let out a shout Tia's well-aimed kick found its mark and he lost his voice.

Waving my arms like Bran's chicken, I pointed to the trees ahead of us and hissed as loudly as I dared, "Go, go, go!" The first trees were only twenty or thirty strides away, but in that moment they could have been across the ocean.

We ran, the six of us, the whole lot of us, without a single thought in mind except to make it to those bowing arms of safety. All my life I had heard of trees. Pippa used them in most of her songs, and every picture she drew in the dusty floor of our cell had a tree in it somewhere. And now, with enemies only strides away, the trees had come to mean escape itself.

From somewhere behind, a young Digger's voice let out a shriek. Within seconds the sleeping soldiers began to stir. A man shouted and helmets all around us began popping up from the grasses. I would have screamed too if I'd had the breath. Pippa was swerving, twisting away from huge grabbing hands and leaping over still-sleeping bodies.

A grinning, toothless face with a fresh cut running down the side of his helmetless head suddenly stood up tall in the grass right in front of me. Leaving Pippa, who was just out of his reach, he concentrated on me. He brought his arms out wide like a crab ready to attack. I gasped and tried to cut more sharply to my right, but my leg wouldn't hold me.

The soldier laughed harshly and swung his arms down. I ducked, tripped, and fell awkwardly, staring up at him from my backside. Suddenly a rock the size of my fist bounced from his chest and landed in the grass near my foot. His twisted grin turned into a grimace and his grasping arms clasped the front of his war tunic in pain. Tia ran past me, calling over her shoulder, "Faster! No rocks left!" I scrambled past the soldier on my hands and knees, then ran on. Only strides ahead, Pippa was entering the trees.

The trees! When the first branches of an enormous gnarled trunk brushed against my face, I couldn't hold back a sob. Wide, green leaves like the fronds of the seaweed on our beach brushed against the top of my hair as I entered the woods. Shadow, soft earth, and filtered sunbeams threw me into confusion for a moment as I tried to find my friends in the gloom.

"Corki!"

I followed Pippa's bobbing back, losing sight of her from blink to blink as the trees began to grow more thickly together. I couldn't see Tia. Bran gave a yelp beside me and changed direction toward the left. Too terrified to look, I tried to weave closer to each trunk as the crashing sounds behind me grew louder. A wall of trees, with their branches tightly knitted together, appeared ahead. Pippa waved frantically at me before plunging through them. Throwing my hands up to push aside the prickly fingers, I plowed through, ducking, lunging, and tripping over the forest floor.

Through the clinging branches we crashed, not caring about where we were going anymore, only trying to get farther away from the danger behind us. Our thrashing cut out the shouts of angry soldiers, and for the moment Pippa led us like a wild thing, heedless of the sharp sticks that cut our feet.

At last she stumbled and fell, taking me down with her near the base of an ancient trunk. I threw my arms out to soften the blow and landed half on top of her. Her heart was beating so strongly I could feel it thumping against my chest. I squeezed my eyes shut.

There was a terrible noise coming from either side of us. But not a single scream or shout. We lay perfectly still, clinging to each other and waiting for soldiers to break through. The crashing grew fainter and then stopped altogether. A light wind filtered through the thick trees and blew against the back of our heads. I smelled the sea.

"I'm so scared," Pippa whispered.

"Me too." I tightened my grip on her waist and lifted my head, listening. Several strange birds screeched above us and their calls were answered by others from the surrounding branches. "Where are they?"

She reached out, lifted a fallen leaf and brushed it across her cheek. "Maybe we aren't worth chasing," she said.

No sooner had she spoken than a loud crackle sent the blood pounding through me again. A booted foot stopped no more than four strides from Pippa's leg. Too frightened to look up, I stared at the hard leather, hoping our silent prayers would be heard. When the man shouted, I bit my lip and felt Pippa's whole body jerk. He yelled again in a commanding voice. This time his call was answered by several others. Then he grunted and shifted his weight to the other foot as if balancing a heavy weapon. I ran my tongue along the edge of my lip, tasting blood and waiting. As if finally satisfied there was no one around, the soldier grunted one more time before moving off in a direction away from the wind. The other voices followed until their heavy steps faded from the woods.

After many, many heartbeats the sun was low enough in the sky to slant beneath the branches overhead and break onto the forest floor.

"I hate the hiding," I whispered finally. Some stick

or rock was digging into my side and I needed to stretch my leg. "Let's sit up." Pippa nodded. Slowly we untangled so that I could put my back up against the trunk.

Pippa lay against my chest and sighed. "Ah, trees."

There were hundreds of lines running down the wood on either side of me, like the rippled sand of the beach. It felt good to rub my hands over the roughness of the bark. The air was cool on my face and the strong, old wood against my back made me feel just a little safer. "I like them too."

It was dark when Pippa stirred me awake. She gripped my wrist.

"What is it?"

Her hand crept up my chest and clamped over my mouth. I sat forward from the tree and listened, aware of the breeze blowing her hair into my face and the scraping of tangled branches. And then another sound rose above the wind. A cough, somewhere to our left, sent chills down my back. I put my hands in front of Pippa's face, making use of the little moonlight there was, and signed *Outside?* She shook her head no. We waited, perfectly still, ready to leap away. The wind fell to a bare breath, and the secret noises of the forest returned.

Another cough, this time to our right. I turned Pippa's head so that she would look at me.

Spears?

Even in the dim light I could make out the flash of her teeth. Two more coughs from our left and then another directly behind had me turning faster than a fish. There was a crackling of dead branches.

"Pippa!" I hissed, tensing up.

She pressed my legs to the ground. "Wait." Then she lifted her hands to her mouth. She coughed. After a brief silence several coughs broke out all around us like an echo in the caves, and then fell silent again.

"I think it's all right," she said quietly. A moment later someone released a loud belch and giggles erupted throughout the trees.

"Idiots," I muttered.

Pippa gave a happy laugh. "We are safe. Outside must have given up."

I could smell Thief before I saw him. Two shining eyes peered out from the darkness, followed by wide, white teeth. "Heh, heh. Coreeko. Pippa."

I held my nose. "You stink, Thief. You're drowning out the nice woods." But I didn't mind even a little when he and Feelah pushed into our tiny forest nest and sat down beside us. There were so many sticks in Thief's hair that if he stood perfectly still he could have passed for a tree. Pippa and Feelah clasped arms.

The Diggers were getting braver and their whispering was beginning to sound like the morning conch in my ears.

"This is not good," I grumbled. "Let's crawl away from here."

"No," Pippa said. "We must find Tia and Bran. Then we will decide what to do."

Frustrated, I got Thief's attention, pointed out into the blackness, and signed *Silence.* He nodded and said something to Feelah. Her face bobbed as she listened. I watched as she stood and whispered quite loudly into the forest.

"Uh-oh," I said.

"What?"

"I tried to tell Thief that the Diggers need to be quiet, and now Feelah is almost yelling into the woods." I grabbed at her work-cloth to make her sit down, but she only smiled and nodded. I was about to pull at her more firmly when she did it again, changing the call into a deeper, jabbering sound very much like the way Thief spoke.

Pippa sucked in a breath. "She speaks other languages!" To my shock, the whispers died down until there was not a hint of anyone other than the four of us sitting among the trees.

Thief stood up beside his mate and whispered in her ear. Then he turned back to us and knelt, tugging at my arm.

Come, he signed.

Pippa hesitated. "What about Tia and Bran?"

We couldn't tell if Thief understood the names. He shook his head. *Come, look.*

"Let's just go see what he wants," I said softly. "He's been right every time so far." I got up with their help, but had to wait for my head to stop reeling. "Wait a heartbeat,

Thief," I groaned. "The stars are still spinning." He led us far more quietly than when we had first entered the forest. I gripped Pippa's hand tightly.

"He knows where he's going," she said. "It is where they must have been hiding before they found us. Let's hope Tia and Bran are near."

No more than fifteen strides away Thief suddenly stopped. Feelah coughed and the sound was repeated a moment later. Leaves rustled. A tall shadow stepped past him and before I could get my own arm back for a punch, long arms wrapped around me, breaking my hold with Pippa.

"Hello, my brave Coriko," Tia whispered. "Twice we have met in strange places and twice I am the happier for it." She reached out next for Pippa, and in a moment Bran was joyously thumping my back.

"We are out, Coriko," he cried in as hushed a voice as Bran could manage. "We are free."

I couldn't help smiling.

"Shhh. Not yet," Tia hissed. "I won't feel safe again until we are far away from here." I could sense her shudder from a whole stride away.

"What should we do?" I asked.

She whispered again. "I think we should stay in the forest. Not here, though—we should move on, we are still too close to the road. And go *quietly*!"

"But we don't know where we are going."

"And what about all the others?" Bran asked. I was about to agree with him when Pippa spoke up.

"They will follow and Feelah can help. They understand her—or at least some of them do. I think Tia is right, we should stay in the forest. But let's also find the ocean. We can see better and find out what is all around us."

With Tia leading we turned our faces into the breeze, toward the sea. It was slow going at first, with prickly branches sticking into our shoulders and flicking at our heads. More than once I heard Bran curse as a branch from the others slapped him in the face.

The signal for Silence was handed from the front to the back so often I lost count. But Pippa was right. The Diggers fell in behind us and when the wind picked up closer to the water, I could barely hear them above the creaking branches.

After a while the trees began to spread out and there

was soft grass under our feet again. I put a hand on a trunk as we passed by to steady myself, and noticed that these were a different sort from those we had hidden under. The bark was smooth like skin and there was a sweet smell in the air around them.

"I know these smells," Pippa sighed dreamily.

Tia and Thief came to a halt. "We should stop here," Tia whispered. "We have come far enough away from the road and the trees are getting thinner. It would not be good to be in the open when daylight comes."

Feelah told the Diggers to lie down. Those who didn't understand followed the rest as we settled for the night on the lovely grass. A huge tree—the kind with the smooth skin, with leaves the size of my hands—made a roof with its puffy branches, hiding the night sky from our sight.

Tia chose to stay awake and watch for danger. "Go to sleep, Coriko," she said when I protested. "You have done enough for now. You've hardly slept for days."

Pippa snuggled up close and the warmth of her back and smell of her hair brought a little comfort. "This is a place of peace," she said softly.

"This is a place of peace," I repeated. But I lost the

rest of her prayer breathing in the air around the tree. "Something smells good." I sniffed at something nearby and my empty stomach rumbled. As I fell into an uneasy sleep my last thought was that it was a good thing Thief had curled up downwind.

10

TRY THIS ONE." PIPPA HANDED me a round shape with almost no holes in it. I took a bite.

"It's good," I said, letting the juice run down my chin. "It's better than that other kind." I pointed to a nearby tree. The trees had turned out to be far more rewarding than just smelling nice. They were loaded with fruit. Some fruit was on the ground, but most was still on the branches. In the night I had dismissed the lumps as part of the forest floor. At first light Tia had woken us up and Pippa surprised us with the discovery.

"Can you walk today, Coriko?" Bran sat next to me.

I stared down at the blood-crusted work-cloth around my leg. "I can walk."

As he helped me to my feet the wind suddenly shifted and he lifted his head. "Something's burning."

I sniffed and smelled smoke. Others had noticed it too. Soon a crowd began to form around Tia.

"Time to go," she said. Pippa slipped an arm under my shoulder.

We traveled in silence, no more than three side by side, like a line of ants coming to clean a crab carcass above the high tide line. Within a very short walk I glimpsed the horizon on our left through overhanging branches. A little farther along, the trees stopped for a stone's throw and we stepped into a wide open space where the long green grass reached to my knees under a brilliant sun. Bees buzzed in the warmth and four or five darting birds chased one another over the top of the field.

"What are those?" Bran whispered, pointing to a collection of stones arranged along the ground ahead of us.

I squinted. "I don't know."

There were quite a few of them. As we approached I could see that someone had put them into a nice order. Each stone was placed one stride away from the others beside it, and two strides in front and behind.

Pippa suddenly shivered, released herself from me and spread her hands out, as if she were feeling the air above the ground. She stepped ahead of Tia, reached the stones before us and knelt down in front of the largest one. I had never seen any rock like it. In the caves the stone was smooth, worn by water, and all the same color. This was cut into a shape with sharp edges and speckled black and white, with tiny flashes of silver. As I stared at the other slabs around us, the sun sparkled off each one. There were symbols carved on most of them and I glanced nervously at the nearest trees. The Diggers were uneasy too, and while a few of them dared to touch the sparkles, most of them hung back.

Tia straightened. "This is a graveyard."

"What is that?"

"It's a place where people bury their dead," she murmured.

I pulled away. "There are *dead* people under these?"

Bran nodded. "And there are even more over there." We followed Bran's pointing finger to a cluster of trees off to the right, where I could barely make out the tips of gray stone hiding in the shade. "Quite a few, too. This must belong to a very old village . . . or a very big one. Maybe even both. Our graveyard is tiny."

Pippa hurried over to the other stones.

"Be careful," Tia called after her. "We must not be seen!"

Eyeing the woods warily, we followed her to the new group of slabs. I could see that there were far more here, smaller and more like the dull rock of Grassland. None of them sparkled, and the symbols were not as well made as those in the field.

Pippa was getting excited. "Come quickly!"

We hurried over to stare at a dirty slab between her hands. Her fingers had whitened at the knuckles as if she meant to lift it from the earth. It looked ready to crumble with age.

"I can read this!" Her wide eyes turned up to mine. In the silence that followed we stared at the familiar symbols etched with painstaking care in the face of the stone.

"'Kirta. Short life, well loved,'" Pippa read solemnly.

Bran scratched his head. "I knew a Kirta in our village."

"It is a common name," Tia said. "But why is it *here*?"

"Here is another," Pippa whispered. "And look, someone brought flowers." I stared at a patch of ruined color at her feet.

"It says 'Kipkar. Hus—husb—'"

"'Husband,'" Tia finished. "That means he was her mate."

"Husband . . . and father." Pippa frowned.

I leaned a little closer to the stone. "These ones are not as good as the ones in the field. They must have run out of the better rocks."

Tia shook her head. "In our village, only the important people can afford a good headstone. The poor just do the best they can."

Silly, I thought. What was the point of putting someone in the ground? In Grassland, when Diggers died the Spears simply threw them into the ocean. The odd one came back, but for the most part they sank.

Tia pointed back to the way we had come. "Those stones are for the rich or the powerful ones in a village. These"—she touched the slab in Pippa's hands—"are for the poor. And there are a lot more of them."

"Yah, Coreeko!" Thief waved. He pointed to a stone

two over from Kirta's. Feelah was squatting in front of it and following the strange symbols with her finger. She looked at us and nodded.

Tia put her hands to her face. "I didn't know our people traveled this far . . . but why would they be buried with others?" She glanced back toward the mountain. Then she focussed on Pippa.

"Could they be Diggers?" she whispered. "Who else would use our writing?"

Pippa shook her head. "No . . . That doesn't make any sense . . . But . . ."

"Then who are they?" Tia asked.

Screeches from the Diggers behind us had me spinning around before we could speak any further. Creeping over the grasses and growing every moment, a dark shadow blotted out the sunlight streaming through the branches.

"Arrows!" Bran croaked.

I turned for the woods. "Run, Pippa!" Diggers shot past me, leaping over the slabs or falling down beside them in their haste to escape from the cloud. Thief was beside me in a moment, flinging his arm out to support me.

"Wait!" I yelled. Pippa had not moved. She was still

bent over the slab, and for a terrifying moment I thought she had been hit.

"Pippa!" I screamed. She looked up slowly and held my eyes. "Pippa, run!"

She shook her head, then stood up and gazed back at the field.

"Pippa, what are you doing?"

"It's not a death cloud," she called, as if noticing for the first time that everyone had left her.

"Please come here," I yelled. "Now." She ran her fingers over the stone at her side and reluctantly walked over to us. Thief was breathing heavily even though we had barely run more than twenty strides, and when she was close enough he swung us around, making for the trees. I kept glancing back over my shoulder to make sure she was following, and waiting for the horrible clatter of arrows.

The others were hiding behind a clump of skin trees, staring up fearfully through the branches. Diggers clung to Tia like barnacles.

"There are no arrows," Pippa said. I looked at the pale faces around me.

"What do you mean?"

"It is smoke."

I took a stride away from Thief.

"It is smoke," she said again. Then her eyes shifted to the ground. "The people are all gone. Dead or dying, but there is no one here."

"How do you know, Pippa?" Tia's voice was shaking. She searched my face, but I didn't say anything.

"I just know."

In a lull of the breeze the reek of burning reached us, and gray wisps of smoke suddenly drifted over the grave slabs behind us.

Bran glanced at me, embarrassment spreading over his face. "Well . . . it *seemed* like the arrow cloud. I thought that—"

"Onesie!" I growled at him. But I felt my shoulders relax. Some color came back into Tia's face and she shook herself loose from the gripping hands.

"If there is a graveyard," she said, "then there is a village. It must be what the Outsiders were after down at the beach—to destroy a village." She moved away from the tree. "And if Pippa is right and there is no one around, then it would be wise for us to go look at what is left. There may be water, food, other things that we can use."

Bran hesitated. "What if she is wrong?" He didn't look at Pippa. "What if there are Outsiders still hunting for us in the woods?"

"She's not wrong," I shot back.

Tia ran her hands over the remains of her sweaty braid. Her eyes were dark and hollow.

"I am tired, Bran. I need to rest. I need food and water. If there is a chance of us getting all that somewhere up ahead, then I am ready to try. As long as the soldiers are gone. All those men were heading back somewhere across the desert, not this way. I don't think we are worth enough for them to chase any more than they already have. It's shards they came for, not Diggers. Let us just be wary and trust Pippa." Her brother nodded slowly and gave Pippa an embarrassed grin.

We decided to walk through the field to get to the beach. "Won't we have to get higher before night so we don't get caught in the flood?" I asked.

Tia shook her head. "Maybe, but I don't think so. I have never seen a place like Grassland before. The beach here is much different—it doesn't look like the tides are so high."

Although the forest had been a refuge for the night, I sensed that most of us wanted to find the open sand and feel the free wind on our faces. It also provided the best view if we were going to find the village. I had shivers as we passed the slabs, and with the smoke still hanging like a mist in the air I quickened my pace. When we broke through the last trees and our feet touched the sand I gave Pippa's hand a little swing.

"Much better," I mumbled.

She continued to glance back over her shoulder. "I want to know who Kirta was. And why she is lying there. I feel like we are leaving her behind."

"Come on, Pippa." I tugged a little more firmly.

Even more wonderful than the sand was the sound of water a few moments later, trickling its way to the sea. Ahead of us a narrow stream rushed by, flowing from the woods and spreading like fingers to where it touched the saltwater. Cool air flowed from the forest and bathed our faces.

Without hesitating I charged as fast as my leg would let me into the center of the stream and plunged my head into the icy coolness. Through my dripping hair I could just make out Thief flinging water up to the sky. Bran was lying straight out, holding his nose and trying to keep his whole body under the surface. I stepped on his back and he flipped over, gasping and laughing. The tiny river was soon filled with Grasslanders making more noise than a thunderstorm.

When I couldn't drink any more I flopped onto the sand beside the stream, letting my feet dangle in the water. The work-cloth around my leg had loosened, so I worked the knot out gently, careful not to disturb the healing wound. Fresh blood splattered as the cloth pulled free, and I tore a strip from the bottom, as straight as I could, and tied it around my leg.

Pippa knelt beside Tia. "Would you like another braid? I know your hair hasn't grown very much since the last time but . . . the forest was not very kind to you." The tearstains from our long night of fear were washed clean from Tia's face and she nodded eagerly. I watched her head bob under Pippa's soothing touch.

"What did we find back there?" she mumbled suddenly.

Pippa tilted the bigger girl's head to tuck in a braid. "I can't believe there were Northern symbols. I thought my eyes were seeing wrong. It has been so long since I have seen our letters made by anyone other than me or Corki."

Tia was more alert again. "And there was an order to the graves. Did you see that? Some stones were less important than others, like the ones in the trees."

"Like slaves and masters," Pippa said.

Tia closed her eyes again. "Pippa, did you see any of our letters among the rich stones?"

"No."

"Then maybe they *were* Diggers!" I said.

Tia thought for a moment. "I guess Diggers could be taken out of Grassland at any time, without anyone knowing," she said. "Maybe used as slaves in the village we are looking for."

Bran nodded. "But even so . . ."

"What is wrong, Pippa?" I noticed she had stopped braiding Tia's hair.

She shook her head. "Give me peace, Corki. I am thinking." Her fingers started to work again but I noticed her eyes turning frequently back toward the gravesite, then up to the mountains around Grassland.

She began hesitantly. "I think . . . I think they were Diggers. But just not when they died."

I wiped at a trickle of water running down my nose. "That has no sense to it. What are you saying?"

But she fell silent and wouldn't say any more. Tia closed her eyes.

With our rest over we walked past the stream and down the beach, away from Grassland. An angry sea bird caught my attention above us, and when I looked back I could see the mountain rising high above the forest. Its dark face loomed above the trees like a brooding Spear, and I quickly turned to the beach.

Some distance farther the sand curved sharply to the right and the ocean dipped into the land. Another stream, larger than the one we had played in, gushed from under the hanging roots of two enormous trees. Unlike the fruit trees, these seemed older than the mountain, with their hundreds of thick gnarly roots reaching for the water. There were only three or four branches to each tree and yet they stretched, some upward and some outward, as if wanting to touch both the ocean and the sky.

"I would like to sit up there," Pippa said quietly, reaching to touch one of the long branches above our heads. "I would sit and rest and pray, and never pick another shard again." I pictured her lying snug in the arms of the great tree and smiled. I hoped she would get her wish.

A short distance later one of the Diggers spotted something. She waved her hands in excitement. Her dirty face was a confusion of amazement and fear as she yammered and pointed.

Boats.

They were grounded on the beach a short distance from the stream trees, and even from where we stood we could tell they had been burned. One of them still had some of its pretty orange sail flapping raggedly in the wind, like the remains of a work-cloth on the bones of a skeleton.

We passed the wrecks quietly, staring at the gaping holes and smoldering wood. A small pile of shards sat heaped where the ocean met the beach. Countless others lay scattered along the shore—from many summers of loading onto the decks, I guessed. No one wanted to get too close to the boats, and from the corners of my eyes I could see that everyone was holding hands.

"We are near, I think," Pippa whispered. Her face had gone white.

Over the next rise in the sand we found the village. Thick, black smoke poured over a wall of raised sticks and wafted down over the water. It was built against the forest, although how far back it went was hard to tell with all the smoke. As we got closer I could see that the sticks had once formed a circle around the whole village. It must have taken many people to shape them so straight and pointed. Now they were fallen in places, blackened and broken like a set of smashed teeth.

Tia kept glancing at Pippa, and slowed her pace just a little so that we formed an arrow with the other Grasslanders fanning out on either side. Although there were no signs of life anywhere we moved cautiously, and more than one head glanced upward. Great slabs of rock bigger than those in the graveyard lay on their backs, forming a wide pathway from the beach to a set of gigantic doors.

When my foot touched the first slab I froze and Pippa squeezed my hand tighter.

"Come with me, Corki."

A line of unquenched fire rippled along the top of the ruined doors. I took my steps hesitantly, always keeping an eye on the flame. The villagers had used the giant stream-trees to build the gates, and from the looks of the sidebeams it would have taken three of us to wrap our arms around them. My eyes watered fiercely. But past the gate the blinding clouds of smoke turned into wisps and flew like fading spirits over the far walls. I picked up a still-burning stick and held it like a prod.

Stone and wood lay scattered everywhere. We stepped carefully to avoid cutting our feet.

"What are those?" I whispered. There was a long line of cut stones formed into walls, as far as I could see.

"Those are dwellings," Pippa whispered back. "It is where they lived." The remains of most of the dwellings were little more than messy piles of rock. But even destroyed, it was clear that this had once been a beautiful place. There were more colors on the ground and on the walls than I had seen in the underwater gardens where we went swimming. Reds, greens, purples shone from torn clothes, polished stones, and metals flashing in the sun. A few of the dwellings were very large. Most of the color seemed to come from them.

The line of homes curved like our bay, and the rising smoke revealed an enormous wall of stone in their center, across from the broken dwellings. I caught a glimpse of a perfectly cut door and flaming colors as high as I could throw my stick, before it was swallowed in a waft of white and black haze.

Smaller roads broke from the center and led toward the outer walls of the village, with dwellings on either side of each one.

Tia's shaky voice broke into my thoughts. "Be on guard for any sign of Spears or soldiers. We will need to look everywhere for food. Quickly, too, before it is all ruined." Pippa nodded in agreement. Thief pulled up beside me and I noticed that he was also carrying a stick. So was Feelah.

At first we stayed close together and our arrow shape began to look more like a clump of frightened minnows. But as we spread out down the lines of dwellings the

Diggers began to do their own exploring. Pippa and I walked along the main road until we came to a second path that worked its way deeper into the village. The dwellings here did not seem as ruined as the others, although many had walls caved in or roofs still smoking. We approached a larger home with a crushed wooden door and a scattering of small stones across the opening.

"I don't like being here," I muttered, poking my head into the darkness. Pippa pushed past me, then stopped before she had gone more than two strides.

"What's wrong?" I hissed.

"Nothing. I just can't see yet. It's too dark." We waited, hearing the muffled voices of the others through the walls. It was cool inside and I shivered, shutting my eyes like I did in the caves. A moment later when I opened them, I could see. Colors seemed to be everywhere the faint light in the room touched. If this was a poor house, I could not imagine what the rich ones were like.

"Cha—chair," Pippa stammered, pointing at an object. "That is a chair." I couldn't believe how many things the people had been able to keep in here. The rooms were maybe the size of four cells, and yet it looked as if the owners did not have enough space to hold it all. I didn't know the names of most of the things, even the ones unharmed by fire. But Pippa moved slowly, touching everything and naming as she went.

"Oh, Corki, look," she said.

I stared at something that had two tiny arms and legs. The head was missing.

"It's a doll."

"Oh."

"It is for a child."

"What does it do?"

She smiled. "You play with it." She gave it a hug.

Silly.

Farther in I found baskets, most of them overturned, filled with seeds and what Pippa called nuts.

"We should take some of those," she said. "We can eat them."

The rest of the dwelling was so badly burned that we moved onto another, leaving our treasure of nuts outside the doorway to be picked up later. I wanted my hands free to hold the stick.

Three homes farther along we peeked into the door of

a small dwelling with a roof stained red. When our eyes could see in the dark, Pippa's voice came out hollow in the tiny room. "There is someone dead here."

I let go of her hand, swung the stick down and gripped it at waist height.

"You won't need that," she said. I peered over her shoulder. It was a woman lying facedown on the floor, with her arms twisted underneath her.

"Let's leave, Pippa."

"No."

"Please, Pippa." When her shoulders began to shake I pulled away and made for the door, but her voice cut me off.

"Corki, wait . . ."

"I don't like it, Pippa."

"I know," she whispered. "But it *is* a Mother."

Mother.

"What?"

"She is a Mother, Corki. Look, she is still holding her baby's blanket."

My head was reeling. "I'm leaving now, Pippa."

"Help me turn her over."

My hands started to shake and I wanted to run outside and yell, or wrestle wildly with Bran. "No."

"Corki."

I turned back but kept my eyes shut, feeling the floor with my stick until I reached her. She shook my arm.

"Open your eyes."

"No."

She gave a little gasp, trying to control her tears. My eyes popped open. They traveled slowly down the far wall, creeping along the blackened floor until a crumpled white cloth with tiny yellow lines came into view. My stick fell to the ground. I knelt on the earth floor, hugging my arms tight to my chest.

A Mother. Her hair was longer than Tia's and blacker than night.

"Help me turn her," Pippa whispered. Holding the Mother's head gently, we moved her onto her back and stared at the lovely face. There was a smudge of white ash on her cheek. I touched the cold skin with my finger to wipe it away.

"Why would they kill her?" I asked quietly.

Pippa's eyes were glistening. "Maybe she didn't want them to have her baby."

I couldn't stop a picture of the tall woman in my mind, standing there in the broken doorway, one hand cradling a crying yellow blanket and the other raised up high to stop a blow. She wouldn't have had a chance. Not against the soldiers of Outside. A rage shook me and suddenly I wished that we were back crawling through the fields, and that I had the chance again to strike with a stone.

"It was very evil for her, I'm afraid," Pippa choked out her words.

"Mine . . . mine lay on the ground like . . . like this too," I heard myself say. Pippa glanced up. "But I can't even remember what she looked like." Pippa took my wrist and held both our hands to her cheek. Then she closed her eyes and began to whisper a prayer over the Mother.

"I wish we could put her in the pretty field," she said many heartbeats later. "Perhaps beside Kirta."

I thought of the cold stones and the dead people lying underneath them. "This is a better place, I think. It is her home."

Pippa said we should place her arms on her chest and brush the hair away from her face.

"Wait," she commanded as I reached down. She stood quickly and began searching the floor. When she came back she was holding something long, and round at one end.

"This is a brush." She lifted it to my eyes. It looked like it was made from bone or white wood. I watched curiously as she gently took some of the Mother's long hair and began to stroke it with the brush-thing. The hair gathered together beautifully and seemed to shine in the pale light streaking in from the roof.

"She looks so cold," Pippa said after a while. "Maybe we could put a cloth on her."

"It won't help."

"I know." She found a long, torn robe under the bed and laid it neatly on top of the Mother. As Pippa was moving about I caught sight of the child's blanket again and picked it up. I folded it several times, then slid it under her head.

Pippa smiled. "Now she has her baby with her too."

When we stood up to leave I drove my stick into the

ground in the middle of where the door had been. We didn't take anything.

"Sleep in peace." Pippa raised her hand in farewell.

Smoke drifted lazily out the only window at the back of the small dwelling and flickers of flame licked at the roof as we made our way toward the others. I kept looking over my shoulder at the house with the Mother lying cold in her house-grave, until I heard the voices of Thief and Bran just ahead.

II

THIEF HAD DISCOVERED THE Spears at the far end of the village, near the outer wall of sticks. There were five of them, lying mostly on top of one another as if they had all died at once. I shivered. I didn't much feel like going near them, but Thief kept tugging at my braids.

He pointed to the new dagger he had found. *Come see. Spear. Dead.*

Searching through dead Spears wasn't going to be pleasant, but having a better weapon than another half-burned stick made me turn around in the end. Pippa stayed with Tia at the village center, so Bran joined me for the long limp over.

"What are they doing *here*?" I asked, carefully touching

the end of an arrow. "The mountain is way back there." It had never occurred to me that Spears could be anywhere else. I gathered that Thief had searched the bodies quite well already. There was no way we could get a better look without turning them all over or untangling the arms and legs. Bran's face was green.

"I don't want a dagger that bad," he gasped. "Can we go?"

It would not have been too much trouble to get a knife off one of them, especially if all three of us worked at it. Among the tangle, pieces of metal glinted in the light. It was difficult to tell what was a weapon and what was armor. I reached in for what might be a knife handle, but my fingers froze as I almost had it. The Spear at the bottom of the pile was missing his mask. Whether it had been knocked off in battle or taken by Outside I did not know, but the eyes were sightlessly staring past my foot. The face made me back away. His right brow was smeared with crusted blood that had trickled down the cheek.

I pointed to a cast-off garment beside the Spears. "Give me a piece of that cloth," I told Bran.

"What are you doing?" He scrunched his face as I leaned toward the dead flesh.

"Get me the cloth!" I hissed furiously, as if our voices might wake them.

There was a shredding sound and Bran pressed something into my hand. I spat on the rag until it was wet, then slowly reached forward. I got to my knees, half expecting the bodies on top to begin reaching their cold hands toward me. As the blood wiped away from the skin, the Spear's face became more clear. My fear grew stronger.

"I—I know him," I croaked.

The Spear did not look as I had last seen him, but there was no mistake. Thief sensed something was wrong and took hold of my shoulder.

"Look!" Bran gasped.

The Spear's mouth suddenly opened, and an unearthly groan erupted at our feet, rising to fill the air around us. We stared, horrified, gripping each other for support. Thief dropped his stick. It clattered loudly against the stones, and without looking back we fled.

We found Pippa and Tia loading baskets and clothes

into the open arms of Diggers at the entrance of a large dwelling.

"Are you *sure*, Corki?" Pippa said, setting her burden down. Tia swatted at a couple of noisy Diggers beside her so that she could listen.

I could barely keep my arms from shaking. "Yes. I knew him. He is much bigger now, but it is him. He was taken about two Separations ago. White Eye, the one with the white eyebrow. Remember? You used to get mad at me for making fun of him." I traced above my own eye. "There is something else, too. . . . It is difficult to see, but he has a red mark on his chest—the red fist, Pippa. He is from the caves."

She trembled and looked at Tia. "A Digger dressed in a Spear's armor . . ."

Tia had stopped midway through lifting a basket of dried fish. "And he is alive?"

I shrugged. "Barely. He made a noise."

She scowled and looked at Pippa. "We'd better come and look."

We gathered as a large group once again and moved slowly back to the far side of the village. The younger

Diggers latched onto Tia the moment it became clear what we were going to see.

The Spears were as we had found them, silent and unmoving. A single crow was perched on the shaft of the arrow I had touched. It squawked angrily at our approach. Clacking its beak along the shaft, it rocked from side to side in protest. I waved my arms to frighten it away. The Diggers had become so quiet that the sound of the bird's wings beating its retreat to the top of the nearest dwelling was frighteningly loud.

Ten strides from the Spears I led the others around the tangle of bodies to where White Eye could be more easily seen. He had closed his eyes. The crow continued to rage at us from above, and I considered finding a good stone to end the noise. Thief gripped the back of my work-cloth so hard I had to keep pulling it off my neck to breathe.

"There he is." The words strangled in my mouth.

I watched as Pippa and Tia went down on their knees. They did not say anything at first, watching to see if White Eye would do anything.

"You are sure you recognize him?" Tia asked.

Pippa nodded.

The older girl reached out her finger and poked the forehead lightly. There was a groan like we had heard earlier. Most of the Diggers took a step back.

"Peace," Tia growled. She wiped the sweat from her own brow.

Pippa touched his nose, then patted his cheek. "White Eye," she called softly.

"Pippa," I started, "do not—"

White Eye blinked. Both of his eyes opened and he let out another agonized groan.

My teeth clamped shut.

"Can we move the others off him?" Tia asked. "He is trying to breathe." Although his arms were clearly trapped beneath him, Tia was taking no chances. She balanced on one knee, ready to spring away.

After our brief attempt to untangle the limbs, White Eye gasped so loudly I thought he was gone for good. "We cannot move them without killing him," I said.

Pippa touched the white scar along his eyebrow. "What are you doing here, White Eye?" she asked.

Trickles of sweat slid off his nose. He glanced briefly at her face, then beyond her to where the rest of us stood waiting.

The weight of the Spears on top of him must have been agonizing, but there was more fear in his eyes than pain.

"We won't hurt you," Pippa said gently. "Why are you here? You are far from Grassland."

He raised his head slightly, almost as if to see if there was a way out above the bodies on top. Thick muscles strained out from his neck, and again I was reminded that he no longer looked like a Digger. He tired quickly, though, and his head slumped.

"You should not do that," Pippa said. "It will only make you feel worse."

A heartbeat later he was at it again. I wondered if he was trying to push the Spears off himself. But his effort did not last long. After the last try, what little strength he had left could only keep his eyes open.

When his man's voice spoke, a shiver ran through my bones.

"Why do you not kill me?" he gasped.

Tia glanced at me, then back to White Eye. "Why would we kill you?"

His eyes flickered for a moment. "I am a Spear."

"But you are a Digger," Pippa said patiently. "We saw

you. You even spoke to us a few times, back in the grasses, remember? More than two summers ago."

His breath rattled and caught in his throat. When he spoke again I had to get on my knees, like the others, to hear.

"Yes," he croaked. "A Digger."

"And now you are a Spear?" Pippa continued to speak softly. "You became a Spear after the Separation . . . ?"

I stared at Pippa. "What are you saying? It is White Eye. *Look* at him."

Her eyes flickered toward me but they never left the groaning man.

"It was *at* the Separation," she whispered again.

This time White Eye seemed to be aware only of Pippa. "Yes."

I could hardly keep from hissing my words. "But *why*? Why would you *do* that?"

"Be gentle, Corki," Pippa warned.

I scowled at her. "Become a Spear?"

White Eye's voice was a low whisper now. His eyes fastened on mine with the coldness of the ocean at morning. "So would you."

If I had not been so frightened I would have spat in his face.

"What did he say?" Bran asked me. He looked too scared to come any closer.

"He said that I would become a Spear too."

"He must have hit his head."

"Why did you not run?" Tia asked, ignoring us. "Avoid the Separation."

He continued glancing from one face to another, uncertain. Then he ran his tongue over cracked lips and his face for the first time looked more like a Digger's than a soldier's.

"C–can't. There are leaders . . . r–rules . . . If I refuse, my mate . . ." With each word his face grew ashen, and I wondered if he really knew what he was saying anymore.

"He needs some water." Pippa stared at me.

I glared back. "He is a Spear."

"Yes," she said. "He is a Spear."

Grumbling, I rose to my feet.

"Wait," Tia commanded. "White Eye is speaking again."

White Eye was no longer looking at any of us.

Instead he stared out at the blackened walls of his village. Beads of sweat rolled down his chin. His cheek twitched uncontrollably.

"My mate," he whimpered. Then he sucked in a deep breath and lay still.

"Where is she?" Tia asked. "Where are the others? Are they coming back?"

He did not speak again. Pippa reached out and closed his eyes. Looking up at us she said, "He is dying now. We should be quiet. I will wait with him until he is finished." A tear ran down her face.

I turned away, angry that she would cry over a Spear.

Tia got up slowly, looking shaken. "You should not wait alone. Some can stay. The rest of us should move back to the center of the village."

For the second time that day I left the side of a dead person. Only this time Pippa did not come with me, and for a Spear I would not drive a stick into the ground.

Later, Pippa told me that White Eye died not long after we left his side. I did not ask her if she prayed for him.

12

AT SUNSET WE ALL SAT AROUND a large collection of food in the middle of the main road, with the dwellings on one side and the wall of sticks on the other. I helped myself to a sack of dried fish, bigger and more tasty than anything we had ever been given in Grassland. But while our food supply had grown, I noticed something else getting smaller. The group of Diggers who now munched on fish and fruit was not the same size as when we entered the village.

"Where are the others?" I nudged Tia.

She frowned. "There are no more Spears, Coriko. Not ones that are alive. The Diggers are doing what they want to do. Some will stay, others will go." She gave an exhausted sigh. "We don't even know what we are going to do next."

Thief had given me his dagger to cut a new cloth for my leg. I felt the heavy metal end and balanced it in my palm. The blade was painfully sharp. It took me only a moment to realize that it was made of shard. I thought of the countless black shards scattered at the beach and wondered how many weapons could be made from them . . . or had already been made from them.

"I wish I could have had one of these in the caves," I grumbled. Yet even this discovery did not answer more burning questions in my mind. "I do not understand why White Eye is a Spear. How could this place be his home?"

"Perhaps they lived here *and* in Grassland," Tia said. "We know from the tunnels there are more places inside the mountain than we have seen."

Pippa rubbed a piece of fruit with a cloth. "It is hard to think when I am so tired. It feels like we are seeing new things every moment, and there is no time to understand it." She glanced at me. "But it does seem as if you may be eating Spear food right now."

Grimacing, I fell back to cutting the cloth and worried

about the night to come. Shadows were growing in the village and I longed to be away from all the burning.

Pippa sensed my mood. "Let's enjoy what we have, Coriko. Questions later." Lifting a cloth by her feet, she handed me something white and lumpy. "Here, try this."

I sniffed at it. "Smells as bad as Thief."

"It is called cheese."

As darkness set in Tia ordered a fire to be made. All the remaining Grasslanders crowded around the flames, sitting on sacks of food and broken pieces from the dwellings. There was a brief argument about having a fire, but as Tia reminded us, the village would continue to smolder for many days yet. The smoke from our small flames would pass unnoticed to any watching eyes.

"We should not be here long, though," she said quietly, leaning back so that Pippa could finish her braiding from the afternoon. "We should go to the safety of the stream and woods again."

"I would feel better there," I said. "The stream is fresh and I trust the trees."

She agreed. "Tomorrow we can come back and carry

the rest of the gathered food. It should be safe from flames until then."

Bran let out a loud belch. "I don't know. I like it here. There are still a few houses I haven't been in yet. We might find some good things. I wish I could find a shard-knife like Thief's." He seemed to have forgotten his uneasiness.

Pippa squirmed. She had been quiet since returning from White Eye, and I was surprised to hear her speak. "I would feel better if we left the Spears alone. I don't think we should steal from them."

"Why?" I tossed a stick on to the flames.

"They are dead. Yesterday they lived and breathed like us, maybe even laughed."

"They were *Spears*, Pippa."

"What about White Eye? What about him? Was he just a Spear? And Kirta?"

"Kirta was not a Spear."

She didn't say anything.

Tia sat up straight and scanned the darkened dwellings around us for a moment.

"I agree with Pippa," she said. "I think we should leave the dead Spears alone. After what we found today, I don't doubt that this was their village. And when I look at this place, the rich houses and poor houses, the two different graveyards, the ships . . . it makes me feel like there is more to understand than what we know. I'm not so sure I hate them anymore . . . I am just not sure why." She gave Bran a long stare. "We don't need anything from them. Let us leave them to sleep in peace. We can take the food and clothes to the stream. Then we can decide what to do next."

Her brother shrugged.

It sent my head spinning to think that we were sitting in the center of a Spear village. "What happened to the rest of the people?" I asked, thinking out loud. "I mean the women . . . and the children? White Eye never said."

Pippa's eyes shifted to me ever so briefly, then returned to the flames. "We found a Mother in one of the dwellings," she said to Tia.

"Oh."

Bran shot me a glance. I pulled a face at him and he looked away.

"Well"—Tia took a deep breath—"maybe their people were taken along in the carts, like the shards. Or perhaps they went in the boats—you said there were many ships.

That makes the most sense to me. The Spears would stay to fight, so their families could escape by water."

A sudden spark shot a spray of ash into the air.

"Or maybe Outside threw them all in the sea," Bran said.

Pippa gave him a glare. I did too. It was ugly for Mothers to be dropped into the sea.

"They probably didn't, though," he added hastily.

Pippa finished with Tia's braid and faced her. "How long until we go to the stream?" she asked.

Tia looked a little surprised. "Soon. Maybe when everyone has finished eating."

Pippa nodded, then turned to me. "Come with me, Corki."

"Where?"

"Just come. We'll be back before it's time to go."

"Don't go far," Tia warned, "and beware of soldiers."

Pippa raised me to my feet, then slipped her hand mysteriously behind her back as she led us away from the others toward the ruined gates. I stopped at the giant doors. The flames had died to a glow, but it was enough to see that her smile hadn't left.

"Where are we going, Pippa?"

She gave a tug. "To find some moonlight."

I groaned. "Is this about woman things again?"

She laughed and walked us in the direction of the beach. Turning to the left toward the stream-trees, we followed the bend, feeling the cool sand under our feet. It was strange to walk outside at night. There was no roof, not even trees. The feel of Pippa's hand was happy, maybe even excited.

And then, just past the creaking broken boats, we suddenly found her patch of moonlight. It lit up her face and sent a pathway of light across the sea to the horizon. Around the bright moon the evening stars had come out to play, tiny torches like Pippa's shimmering eyes. She stopped, breathing deeply.

"Close your eyes and do not open them until I tell you."

I shut my eyes. There was a rustling sound and a long pause before she spoke again. "Open."

Standing in front of me was a young woman. She was dressed in a long cloth, of a color I couldn't make out under the moon, but it was brighter than those I had seen in the village earlier. Her hair hung down onto the cloth, not plaited behind her head like a Digger's, but free and wild like the wind.

"Pippa?"

She laughed. "Woman clothes, Corki! I found them today."

I approached her awkwardly.

She laughed again. "Do you like it?"

I touched the cloth gently. "You look like . . . like a woman," I said finally. "A *young* woman." Before I could say anything more she jumped at me, sending us crashing to the sand. Despite the pain it was good to have my old Pippa back. I was just about to tell her so when she leaned down and kissed me. Not on the nose, not on the cheek, but on my lips.

"Is this what you and Tia talk about?" I asked when she pulled away. She leaned down and kissed me again, this time for a little longer.

"I like that," I said. She put her head on my stomach and together we looked up at the shimmering lights of night outside Grassland.

Some time later her hand started to drum the sand.

"What are you thinking?"

"I think I know a secret," she said.

I lifted myself up to my elbows. "Hmmm?"

Both her hands were drumming now. "Where would you go if they took me away from you—during the Separation, I mean?"

"I *wouldn't*! I would stay . . . I would . . ." I leaned over her. "What are you talking about?"

She lifted a finger and touched my nose. "I was thinking of White Eye. What if he was in a Spear's clothes because he *had* to be?" She chose her next words carefully. "I know that Thief would die for Feelah. And you said Tia took a prod in the stomach to help Bran. So . . . maybe White Eye was a Spear because something worse would happen to him if he wasn't." She paused then, talking more to herself than me. "All our lives we have wondered what would happen at the Separation. We have feared it more than a First Cleansing."

I nodded.

"And now, perhaps White Eye has shown us the answer . . . White Eye and all the other Spears with the red fist on their chests." Once again she hesitated, lowering her eyes as if she could not look at me and still say the words.

"What, Pippa?"

"What if . . ."

"Tell me."

"What if Diggers have no choice? What if they *have to* become Spears?"

Words stuck in my mouth. The ocean, so close to us, continued to fill the air with the sound of its crashing, as if nothing had changed. Yet I felt no comfort.

Pippa watched me closely, our eyes meeting and holding, while images of Diggers, Spears, shards, gravestones, and White Eye all tumbled about inside my head.

And then a vision of dead Spears lying all over the mountainside turned my stomach with a horrible wrench. I wondered what we might find if their helmets were taken off. The idea of one of those terrible frowning masks one day being forced over my own head almost choked me.

"That is a—*terrible* idea, Pippa."

"I didn't say it was true. I said, 'What if?'"

I thought of the cold gravestones and the Northern letters cut crudely into the rock. Had some Digger-turned-

Spear carved his son's or daughter's name years after a Separation?

I scratched my head. "But *why* would Diggers become Spears? I never would!"

She nodded. "White Eye said something about not being able to run away, that there were leaders and rules. And he was worried about his mate." Her tapping grew stronger. "I think at the beginning they are forced to become Spears. But then . . . maybe over time . . . they choose it for themselves." She raised her eyebrows. "It is a nice village . . ."

"Choose it?" I said. "*Choose* being a Spear?"

She smiled. "Only two days ago you did not want to talk about escape. Do you like being a Digger?"

"That is different."

"Why?"

"Because Diggers are Diggers and Spears are Spears."

"Yes!" She clapped her hands. "And when you have become a Spear, all you do is be a Spear."

I shook my head.

"Corki, would you become a Spear if it meant we could stay together? If it was the *only* way?"

I didn't hesitate. "Yes." Then slapping the sand I said, "And so would Bran . . . and Thief. And probably the rest of those idiots back there too." I pointed toward the village and our fireside. "I would die to stay with you."

"So would they," she said softly. "So would they, for their mates."

"Yes."

She tilted her face to the sky. "But we would be a different kind. A new kind. We would try to be Spears who protected Diggers."

The waves sounded a little closer and this time I felt their soothing song.

"What about Mothers?" I said.

"And Mothers."

She smiled her beautiful smile. "Can we try the new kiss again?"

On our way back to the village I held her more closely than usual. "Do I have to wear man clothes from now on?" I asked.

"No. But I would like to see you in them at least once."

We heard Tia's voice calling long before the light of the

campfire could reach us through the gates. The sound of a Threesie using our names gave me a warm feeling all over. Pippa stopped and listened to Tia's voice.

"My mother used to do that," she said. "Call me to come in at night."

We helped the others pack and carry the food. The last glow of the village fires was swallowed by the forest as we marched into the night. It was a long walk to the stream-trees and the darkness should have held little fear for us. Even so, I kept my fists ready to fight and searched the woods constantly. My leg hurt with each step. When the welcoming sound of the stream greeted us, I felt an enormous weight fall from my shoulders. I looked less often into the gloom and stopped jumping at every sound.

"The night will keep us safe from prying eyes," Tia assured us. "Although I cannot think of who might be out there." She shuddered. "Tomorrow we will build a fire," she added firmly. "And from that time on let no Spear or Outsider put it out!"

Pippa shifted at my side. "There were many Diggers who did not follow us."

I looked at the small, shadowy company clustered around us. “Yes,” I agreed. “Quite a few.”

Tia’s face was hidden in the darkness but I could sense she was looking at me. “Is that a problem?”

“It might be,” I said thoughtfully. “We have most of the food. When the village finally burns down and the food is spoiled, they will come after us looking for more. Stealing is easier than gathering. Ask Thief.”

Tia snorted. “Let them! After all we have been through, I refuse to worry about a ragged band of children.” She was silent for a moment. Then she added, “I am more concerned about Spears or Outsiders returning. When the shards run out, surely the Outside will come back for more. And the Spears? How do we know that *all* are dead? No, Coriko, do not bother me with little Diggers. We must be ready for greater dangers in the days ahead.”

Pippa squeezed my hand so I did not answer our Threesie. My cellmate was right. There would be time enough for worry. For now, the Outsiders had returned to their desert and the Spears were dead. We had food and the shelter of the stream-trees that stood on guard like friendly soldiers. It had become my favorite place.

"You need to rest," Pippa murmured and helped me lie down near the water. "Are you cold?" she asked.

"A little. My leg hurts."

"We need to bathe and clean it to quicken the healing. Although I fear this wound will take some time. Here is an extra wrap from the village." We dipped my leg twice into the chilly water.

Thief was already snoring, stretched out on the soft, mossy ground. Feelah rested against him. Even in the blackness I could see her shining teeth grinning at me. "Rest," she murmured. She often repeated our words, and it had not taken long to realize that she was probably the smartest of all of us.

It was a good place for resting. The moss provided more comfort than the filthy straw the Spears flung into our cells.

"I would like to sleep here every night," I said.

Not far was the sea, its salty flavor mingled with the breeze. I smiled comfortably. Living by the water, the Spears had an endless source of food. And Bran and Tia knew how to fish. I suddenly remembered the fruit trees we had found near the graveyard and my mouth watered.

How good it was to have so much food! At least our little company would never starve.

In the morning Thief could follow the stream to its end, seeking the best hiding places. We would post guards as the Spears had done on the mountain the night Outside attacked. Tia was right: We would not let anyone put out the fires we made. No one would rule us again.

I glanced at my cellmate as she retied the cloth on my leg. Her fingers moved nimbly and gently as always. In the coming days it would be Pippa, I knew, who would show us how to act differently from the Spears. We had our Threesie with us now, but Pippa would lead us in ways of the heart.

The wrap draped the length of my body, its warmth quickly spreading. I closed my eyes. "What is going to happen now, Pippa?" I mumbled. The drone of Thief's snoring and the sounds of others making ready for rest was as peaceful as the tumbling stream. It was good to sleep beside those you could trust.

She leaned her head on my shoulder. "We will all

sleep," she said. "But not for long. Grassland is awake, Corki. Now we must learn to live."

"I like this place," I murmured.

"This is a place of peace," she answered.

ABOUT THE AUTHOR

David Ward was born in Montreal, Quebec, and grew up in the city of Vancouver beside the mountains and ocean. He was an elementary school teacher for eleven years before completing his master's degree. David is currently a writer and university instructor in children's literature. He lives in Vancouver with his wife and three children. This is the first book in a trilogy of Grassland adventures. Visit him online at www.davidward.ca.

THIS BOOK WAS ART DIRECTED by Chad W. Beckerman. The text is set in 12-point Adobe Garamond, a typeface that is based on those created in the sixteenth century by Claude Garamond. Garamond modeled his typefaces on ones created by Venetian printers at the end of the fifteenth century. The modern version used in this book was designed by Robert Slimbach, who studied Garamond's historic typefaces at the Plantin-Moretus Museum in Antwerp, Belgium. The display type is Charlemagne.

Sneak peek from

Book Two of

The Grassland Trilogy

Beneath the Mask

I

IF WE REMAINED QUIET, THERE was a chance some of us could make it to the ship alive.

Pippa squirmed beside me. "Ashes," she mumbled. "Ashes and fire." She tried to sit up, but I pushed her back down until she stopped moving. It did not stop her words from sounding again in my head.

Ashes and fire. It was a recurring dream for her—even more so as the day of our escape drew closer. I glanced above the high grass where the rest of the cellmates lay within touching distance. Some rested, others watched the thicker woods behind us. Against the night sky their gray cloaks and hoods flickered occasionally, like the tree shadows so near. Ahead, drifting in swirls of mist, the outline of a ship swayed against the stars. A brilliant moon, close to full, shone down on our scattered hiding places. Its face played a deadly game with me, lighting up anything that showed itself while making the shadows still deeper. "Ashes and fire," she whispered again.

"Be quiet, Pippa," I hissed.

I pulled my gaze away from the rustling in the woods to look at her. The woman clothing she had taken from the Spear village sat so loosely on her small shoulders, it rustled with the lifting of a finger. I wished again that she had settled for her old work-cloth as I had. Careful not to look at her eyes, I eased my hand away from her.

Her lips tightened. "Corki, if I stood up right now and screamed, it might be no different than what could happen to us later. You must listen to me. And Tia must as well."

I risked a more thorough glance behind, above the short bramble against our backs. Dark trees rose at the foot of the mountain. Its enormous shadow crept all the way to the ocean, and one arm of it, a giant wall of stone to our left, stretched into the sea, blocking our view of the bay. It also hid our secret, the very reason why we lay still as stones, waiting for the morning.

"Do you want them to find us?" I hissed at Pippa. "Do you know what they will do?"

She nodded. "Yes, I know. But I would rather face Strays than something I do not know. They were Diggers once. Just like us."

"But now they are not like us," I growled, "They steal our food and attack at night. This is why we fixed the Spear ship. It is why we are lying here—to escape from them!" Before I could say more, the grasses rustled at my side and a strong hand gripped the back of my hair.

A long shadow moved across our faces. Tia had crept up without me sensing her. "No more talk!" Her dark eyes flashed and her face hardened.

"Tia, listen to me," Pippa whispered. "You must—"

Tia's hand left my braid in a blur and struck Pippa sharply on the forehead, with almost no sound. No one had hit my cellmate before without me striking back. I never imagined Tia being the first to do it.

"Forgive me!" she whispered urgently. "Forgive me. But you must be silent. The Strays are so close. And we are almost away." She caught sight of my raised fist and tears of desperation welled up. "I beg you, be silent. How many have we already lost tonight? Shall I lose you both as well?"

Although Pippa's shoulders shook she did not speak or cry out. Instead she nodded, pressed my hand down, then pushed her face miserably into the grass.

Tia slumped in relief. She reached out and stroked Pippa's hair gently, then risked a few words to me. "Come. Thief is waiting near the beach. Bran can stay with Pippa."

Until that moment I had not realized that her brother lay hidden half a stone's throw ahead of us and closer to the sand. He nodded at my stare. I smiled, hoping he could see. No one was as fearful as Bran, but other than Thief, or maybe Tia, I could not think of anyone who had more courage. It felt good to see him. All night he had worked beside me, keeping the others quiet, and carrying more than his share through the tangled woods. Tia signed for him to join us.

A crackle of branches a moment later made all of us cling to the earth. Bran's head went down. There were no voices, only the slapping of brush against bare skin as the Strays made their way through the undergrowth. It was

difficult to tell exactly how many there were, for more sounds were beginning to mingle as they searched closer toward the beach.

The white undersides of leaves glimmered here and there as the Strays pushed them aside. I felt for a stone, easing it gently from beneath the roots of the tall grasses. Above their tips I thought I could see the flash of eyes. In the dim light, flesh and bone seemed little different from trunk and branch with the wind blowing the forest into life.

When the crashing started again I squeezed Pippa's hand so hard she pulled away. I turned the stone around in my palm to get the best grip. I would aim for the head, one shot only—eyes or nose were best. Bran would have to move closer to take the Strays at the back. I signed *Come.* Beside me, Tia had risen to a crouch, ready to spring at our attackers. I slid to my knees, shoulder to shoulder now between Bran and Tia. Beads of sweat glistened on the back of her hands.

Ten strides away another crashing broke out to our left. I raised my throwing arm. Tia caught my wrist. She shook her head and I peered into the darkness. It was a

Digger this time, one of us, unable to contain his fear any longer. I could hear his sobbing as he ran back into woods. It was a desperate try for escape, but I understood it. The Strays burst forward immediately to start the chase. The woods erupted with shouts.

We sat upright, the four of us, waiting for attackers to break through the grass. Again I raised my arm, ready to strike the first head that showed itself. This close to the chase, I was able to distinguish many footfalls as Stray after Stray landed on a patch of hard soil just strides from our noses. The smell of their unwashed bodies wafted toward us.

We could hear them pushing each other forward, spurring the ones in front to move faster, closer to the hunt. Tia stifled a scream when one of them tripped and a foot slid through the grass, crashing into my knee. As my hand started down toward it, Pippa caught my wrist. The toes crinkled against my skin. Then the foot pushed off to stumble after the other Strays.

Only our eyes moved until the noise gradually became less as the Strays followed their prey back toward the stream-trees. Tia's forehead came to rest against my shoulder. I could feel her sigh on my arm. Pippa was still holding my hand, my rock frozen in the air. My own breath was coming in gasps.

"Let's go," Tia whispered a moment later.

I looked to Pippa, uncertain whether I should be angry or thankful for her silence. I suddenly longed for the peace of our cell where I could speak to her in quiet. "What should I do?"

She did not answer at first. Her eyes, normally so green in the sun, stared back colorless in the dim. "This is all wrong, Corki. But do what you must to help the others. I will wait with Bran." She touched my face. "Only do not be caught. I will not live without you. That much you know."

"I will not be caught."

It hurt like a shell cut to leave her, even for only a short while. There was some comfort entrusting her to Bran, especially with the Strays off hunting for the moment. At least, that is what I told myself as I hunched lower to follow Tia.

Bran gave me a nervous grin from under his hood as we squirmed past him. I pressed my stone into his hand.

"Run toward the ship if you hear anything," I whispered. He nodded.

I followed Tia's heels closely, no longer with the freedom to stand or even crouch. There was less cover away from the trees. Any Strays looking this way from the beach would quickly see us in the moonlight.

The grasses, so close to my nose, drowned out the scent of the woods behind us. They were not as tall here as the grasses in our bay, where the shards lay hidden under deep roots. This was soft and green in the daylight, like the leaves of trees.

The other Diggers stared as we crawled past, their arms wrapped tightly around their bundles—both for warmth and comfort. I hardly recognized any of them, crouched as they were in the grass. Most were wearing gray work-cloths, although here and there I caught sight of color against the pale grass. For the first time in our lives we had things we could call our own. Warm wraps, a comb, even a necklace or two of glittering stones. Some of the Onesies had taken as much as they could carry from our weeks in the Spear village. Now it only slowed them down. I wondered briefly how many of them had considered joining the Strays before this night.

When I suddenly felt sand mixed in among the roots, I crawled faster to catch up with Tia. She stopped, then nodded. A flicker of movement caught my eye. Whether it was a sweep of an arm or a twirl of sand flung up by the wind I could not tell. Had we passed all the Diggers who were with us?

Tia lifted an open palm. *Peace.*

Despite her assurance my fingers trembled as I raised myself a handbreadth to look.

A lone figure lay sprawled as we were, his feet at our faces and his arms pressed to the ground. The crash of the ocean was louder here and the light noticeably brighter. Tia and I made our way up either side of him, so close I could have smelled his breath if the wind were not blowing.

Turning, the thief raised his palm against the sky and signed Peace. I could barely make out the jagged scar running along the inside of his wrist, but I knew it was there. I had been with him when it happened.

"Thief," Tia whispered. "Anything?"

I could feel the rumble of his chuckle. Only Thief

would laugh at a time like this. Although his black eyes were hard to see, his teeth flashed brightly. When he spoke, his accent rose only enough to be heard above the wind.

"No Strays." He pointed toward the ship.

I looked out. From where we lay the beach stretched in front of us like the belly of a long gray snake playing with the lapping water. Other than that, there was not a hint of movement between the mountain headlands in either direction, except for the pounding surf. For a brief moment my hopes rose.

"They are out there," Tia muttered. "Everywhere. I can smell them."

I leaned even closer to Thief. The Strays had a distinct odor from living among the burned and dead things of the Spear village. It announced them long before they could be seen. Ash was thick among the burned dwellings too, and its whiteness made the Strays look all the more frightening by day, and terrifying at night. In the last few days their raids on our food had become more dangerous than before.

They attacked at night in groups of no fewer than twenty and carried stones or pointed sticks. Their eyes would flare in our firelight and their shadows seemed to haunt the trees. Now the daylight had become just as dangerous. Too dangerous to remain.

I spat downwind.

Thief grunted. He shared my feelings. The Strays were traitors, Diggers turned wild who had left us soon after we were out of Grassland. I could still remember them clinging to Tia while we searched the broken houses of the Spear village for food. But when we had gathered enough to eat they began to wander off, greedy to find any of the Spear things that remained after the fires started by Outside had burned the houses to the ground. Strays did not want to share as Pippa taught us to. Instead they had peered at us through broken doorways and smoking walls, waiting for the right moment to steal.

When we had moved to the stream-trees they followed at a distance, under the cover of the leaves and the dark, to find where we would store our food. As more of our company left, the Strays gained in strength and numbers. Although they had no Threesie as we did, a leader rose up among them, one who was jealous of the food we gathered from the trees or the shore of Grassland. In the end, we

decided to escape by boat, using one of the Spear ships still docked in the bay. It took a long time to repair that ship, working late at night and as silently as possible. But there was little choice. It was our only chance.

Tia's voice broke into my thoughts. "It is time," she was saying. "We will get everyone on board, then wait for dawn. As soon as we can see enough to get safely out of the bay without crashing into the rock—" she fixed her gaze on both of us in turn—"we go."

Keep reading! If you liked this book check out these other titles.

Elf Realm: The Low Road
by Daniel Kirk
978-0-8109-7069-4
$18.95 hardcover

Operation Redwood
by S. Terrell French
978-0-8109-8354-0
$16.95 hardcover

Fell
by David Clement-Davies
978-0-8109-1185-7
$19.95 hardcover

Bedford High School
Library

AMULET BOOKS, AVAILABLE WHEREVER BOOKS ARE SOLD | WWW.AMULETBOOKS.C

Send author fan mail to Amulet Books, Attn: Marketing, 115 West 18th Stre New York, NY 10011, or in an e-mail to marketing@hnabooks.com. All mail v be forwarded. Amulet Books is an imprint of Harry N. Abrams, Inc.